CONAN DOYLE MEETS JACK THE RIPPER

A True Story

Kelvin I. Jones

CUNNING CRIME BOOKS

All Rights Reserved. The right of Kelvin Jones to be identified as the author of this work has been asserted by him in accordance with the Copyright, Designs and Patents Act of 1988. No reproduction, copy or transmission of this publication may be made without written permission. 2023

Table of Contents

ACKNOWLEDGEMENTS	v
WHEN CONAN DOYLE MET JACK THE RIPPER	7
STRANGE MEETING.	7
THE RIPPER'S HAND	13
LETTERS FROM HELL AND THE CRIME CLUB	17
THE RIVER THAMES	27
CONAN DOYLE AND CRIMINOLOGY	37
WOMEN AS VICTIMS	43
THE RIPPER'S LOATHING OF 'FALLEN WOMEN'	45
MURDER AND BLOODY MAYHEM	51
THE REAL JACK THE RIPPER	53
PLAY UP AND PLAY THE GAME	67
THE CHIEF SUSPECT: THE FACTS OF THE CASE	71
FURTHER FACTS REGARDING DRUITT AND BLACKHEATH	75
THE CRICKET LINK	79
WHAT WE DO KNOW ABOUT MONTAGUE DRUITT	83
BIBLIOGRAPHY	109
APPENDIX A:	115
APPENDIX B:	119
APPENDIX C:	133

ACKNOWLEDGEMENTS

I am especially aware that, in terms of the literature about The Ripper, "there is nothing new under the sun," to quote Sherlock Holmes. However, I am most grateful to the indefatigable owners of the website, www. ripper.org for their accumulated wisdom and in particular, to their many contributors.

However, my greatest obligation has been to Mr Christopher J. Morley's E-book, 'Jack the Ripper: A Suspect Guide' (2005), whose clear perspective and reasoned argument about the true identity of The Ripper should be widely acknowledged.

WHEN CONAN DOYLE MET JACK THE RIPPER

'You have been in Whitechapel, I perceive...' –

Sherlock Holmes.(Apocryphal).

STRANGE MEETING.

Clearly, Jack the Ripper was by no means a normal person. Conan Doyle, the author of the Sherlock Holmes tales, would have said quite a bit about this criminal but the fact is that he did not. We shall examine why this was later on.

Doyle would have said the Ripper was inspired to do what he did because he was possessed by an 'idée fixe'.

According to the *Encyclopaedia Britannica*,

'In the late 19th century, French psychologist Pierre Janet appropriated the label 'idée fixe' for use in a clinical context. He applied the term to any inflexible and often irrational belief, such as a phobia, typically linked to a traumatic memory, that slips from conscious control (becomes 'dissociated') and subsequently dominates a person's mental activity.'

For example, the eating disorder anorexia nervosa, characterised by self-starvation, would be the outward expression of such an idée fixe. To treat the illness, Pierre Janet submitted, psychologists must address 'not only the patient's aversion to eating but also the idée fixe and the related traumatic experience that lies at the root of the condition'.

According to Dr. Watson, in his account of the story of 'The Adventure of the Six Napoleons', 'There are no limits to the possibilities of monomania'. There is the condition which the modern French psychologists have called the *'idée fixe"*, which may be trifling in character and accompanied by complete sanity in every other way.

A man who had read deeply about Napoleon or who had possibly received some hereditary family injury through the Great War might, conceivably, form such an *idée fixe'* and under the influence of this then be capable of 'any fantastic outrage'. It might be said that in Doyle's classic murder story, Sir Charles Baskerville's obsession with the legend of 'The Hound of The Baskervilles,' resulted in an *idée fixe*, which consequently, though unintentionally terminated his life.

The word *psychosis* was introduced to the psychiatric literature in 1841 by Karl Friedrich Canstatt in his work 'Handbuch der Medizinischen Klinik'. He used it as a shorthand for 'psychic neurosis'. At that time neurosis meant any disease of the nervous system, and Canstatt was thus referring to what was considered a psychological manifestation of brain disease. Ernst von Feuchtersleben is also widely credited as introducing the term in 1845, as an alternative to insanity and mania.

A *psychosis*, is now defined as a mental disorder characterised by symptoms, such as delusions or hallucinations, that indicate impaired contact with reality, a term which now refers to any severe form of mental disorder, e.g. schizophrenia or paranoia, was not in common currency.

This notion of an all- consuming obsession of the type exhibited by the Ripper was a popular one with Conan Doyle and can be seen at work in other non-Sherlock Holmes stories; for example, in his horror story, 'The Brown Hand,' and most of all in his often ignored novella, 'The Parasite.'

Interestingly, for fans of the Holmes stories, it has often been noted that obsession formed also an immense subject for that great originator of the entire crime genre,

Edgar Allan Poe. The most original example of this, surely must be 'The Tell Tale Heart,' wherein Poe vividly conveys the emotional state of intensity of his central character, a deranged psychopath, through the use of a monologue. This form of short story has since become a favourite type of narrative to portray criminals suffering from what psychiatrists would also now be defined as 'a disassociated state of mind.'

A prolific crime writer, Conan Doyle visited Scotland Yard's famous Black Museum along with other writers. In 1968, the Met police moved into their present modern building at 10 The Broadway, London SW, what was known by them before as the 'Black Museum', The Black Museum, thus described, because of the many grim, bloody cases represented in the collection, and the dark nature of many of its artefacts, still to this day houses a unique collection of documents, photographs, and exhibits. These cover a wide range of subjects, including housebreaking tools which once belonged to the burglar and murderer, Charlie Peace, items relating to some of the notorious Victorian railway murders, and those dating from the great London train robbery. There are sections dealing with abortions, and even a tableau of Burke and Hare, whose grim story we now know from his letters, once fired the vivid imagination of young Conan Doyle when his uncle Michael took him to Madame Tussauds. There are also sections on offensive weapons, espionage, and forgeries. In particular, there's a section which deals with district displays concerning particular crimes. There are bizarre items like a loving cup, made from a human skull, and the death masks of the most notorious and famous Victorian criminals.

Several of the skulls that belonged to persons executed, are even to this day on display, their history written about by several 19th Century criminologists like Conan Doyle's friend, Major Arthur Griffiths, who described the lives and bizarre careers of some of these outlandish individuals, especially the 'celebrity' poisoners like Palmer and Pritchard. There are some highly grotesque artefacts for those who feel, in Shakespeare's words, they have not yet 'supped too full of horrors,' including a murderer's severed arms, in a tank of formaldehyde, a skeleton and a pickled brain, plus instruments of death and torture.

Dr Pritchard, the celebrated Victorian poisoner.

The Black Museum contains well over a hundred exhibits relating to 150 years of police history. Many of the artefacts' extensive collection relate to several of the murders and murderers and the museum is now on open access to members of the public, although it is restricted to that of previous inquiries only, since, as one would anticipate, the nature of the exhibits may be somewhat disturbing, as for example, in the exhibits relating to some of the Victorian Ripper crimes.

THE RIPPER'S HAND

'You know my methods. Apply them.'

– Sherlock Holmes.

From our reading of the Sherlock Holmes stories, we know that Sherlock Holmes was an expert on handwriting analysis.

Cyphers, footprints and distinctive marks on paper, plus the effects of a particular livelihood on the hand of a person who pursued his or her occupation; analysis of these and other trace elements were part of the detective's expertise, yet there is little evidence apparent of methods of crime detection like these actually being employed by police when tracking The Ripper. As a doctor, Doyle had been taught in Edinburgh by Joseph Bell FRCSE, a Scottish surgeon and lecturer at the medical school of the University of He is best remembered as an inspiration for the character of Sherlock Holmes.

In his instruction to medical students, Joseph Bell emphasised the importance of close observation in making a diagnosis. To illustrate this, he would often pick a stranger, and by observing him, encourage students to deduce his occupation and recent activities. These skills caused him to be considered a pioneer in forensic science, (forensic pathology in particular) during a period when science was not yet widely used in criminal investigation, for certainly had it been so, in my view, the Ripper would have been apprehended.

In fact, Holmes' knowledge was as wide as was that of his maker, Conan Doyle, and it was also extremely precise. Conan Doyle was a physician and a keen, intelligent observer of his patients' abnormalities.

Doyle was also a most original writer, and when he created Sherlock Holmes, he also imprinted on popular culture the idea that when the elements of science are coupled with applied logic, very often complex crimes and apparently ineluctable crimes can be solved.

Doyle also knew that the way to brand the concept in the public's hearts and minds was to package the science he had acquired in the form of short and frequently bizarre tales, featuring a uniquely fascinating, and dysfunctional man. After all, it had worked before in Charles Dicken's 'Bleak House', published in 1853. In that novel, the rather drab Inspector Bucket personified all that intrigued the public about Scotland Yard detectives and their methods.

It should come as no surprise, therefore, to imagine that Conan Doyle would have solved the Ripper enigma. He was most concerned, as he said in his only reported comment on the Ripper affair, in an interview in the magazine 'Titbits', in 1894, that the police had simply not asked handwriting experts to look at the handwriting examples which had been sent to police and the news agencies and then see if they matched any of the letters that their relatives had produced.

In addition, it does not seem that the police actually compared any of the many newspaper reports about the Whitechapel murders. Yet, Conan Doyle, living as he was during the period of the last murders when he was in the area of Portsmouth in Southsea, would have been able to take advantage of a newspaper called 'The Portsmouth Evening News'. This newspaper published very graphic accounts of the murders and provided immense detail. Therefore, Conan Doyle would have acquired a depth of detail regarding most of the forensic evidence, regarding these murders which in turn, may have revealed to him the true identity of The Ripper.

LETTERS FROM HELL AND THE CRIME CLUB

'I am a brain, Watson. The rest of me is a mere appendix.'
– Sherlock Holmes.

In the December of 1903, following Doyle's exploits in South Africa and subsequent knighthood, a small group of like-minded men who shared an interest in murder, met in London to discuss the formation of a private dining club, dedicated to their mutual interest in discussing crime in general. Thus was 'The Crimes Club' born; these men were treating the subject not with morbid or prurient curiosity in the macabre but with enquiry and enquiry learning about murder and its causes, a phenomenon, and an activity, then largely 'owned' by newspapers, who possessed sensational headlines but who offered little enlightenment to the public.

Shortly after it began, the Club doubled its membership, bringing in Sir Arthur Conan Doyle, then and even now one of its most famous founder members. Membership subsequently grew to twenty, with each man (there were no ladies) being allowed to bring a guest on condition that the proceedings were kept strictly private. This condition (known today as 'observing 'Chatham House Rules') was and remains crucial, thus allowing primary crime sources – barristers, judges and so on, to speak openly about their cases to the members.

Membership continued to grow, bringing such notables as Lord Northcliffe, the newspaper magnate, also a friend of Doyle, and the great legal advocate, Sir Edward Marshall Hall. Like today's Garrick Club, ladies were under no circumstances invited to become members. One pre-war former Secretary of the Club wrote of this prohibition:

'The most fantastic suggestion ever made to me was that we should have a grille and admit ladies behind it. But we speedily rejected this; while repudiating any possible accusation of misogyny, we opined that the fair sex already possessed quite as much knowledge as was good for them'.

On at least two separate occasions, Conan Doyle travelled to London to attend these all male meetings and on one memorable occasion, toured the murder sites of Whitechapel with one of the leading police surgeons.

We know that Conan Doyle analysed the message in the original letter from the Ripper and that it was seen by him at the Black Museum. And we also know that he assumed that the murderer was of foreign extraction, or had lived abroad, possibly for a long time. He also was of the opinion that the man who committed the crimes possibly may have been of American origin. (This was the 'Dear Boss' letter which was sent to the Criminal Agency in the September of 1888.)

There was also a theory at one time which he no

doubt had read which was popular with the ex-commissioner of Police, Robert Anderson: that the Ripper was likely to have been a person of Jewish extraction.

When this information and its accompanying theory by Anderson was leaked to the press, it understandably caused a great deal of hostility among the largely dominant East End Jewish community. Anderson, ostensibly the only person responsible for making this view public, published an article about his theory in Blackwood's Magazine, a journal subscribed to by Doyle (Doyle also submitted stories to it), in March 1910, (Part Six), where he writes as follows;

'One did not need to be a Sherlock Holmes to discover that the criminal was a sexual maniac of a virulent type, that he was living in the immediate vicinity of the scenes of the murders. And he was not living absolutely alone. His people knew of his guilt and they refused to give him up to justice.

During my absence abroad, the police had made a house to house search for him. Murders are rare in London and the Jack the Ripper crimes are not within that category. And if the police investigating the case of every man in the district would know the circumstances were such that he could go and come and get rid of his blood stains in secret. And the conclusion we came to was that he and his people were low class Jews. For it is a fact that people of that class in the East End will not give up one of their number to Gentile justice, and the results proved that our diagnosis was right on every point. For I may say at once that if Scotland Yard had powers such as the French police possess, the murder would have been brought to justice.

'Scotland Yard can boast that not even the subordinate officers of the department will tell tales out of school. And it would ill become me to violate the unwritten rule of the service. The subject will come up again. And I will only add here that the Second Ripper letter, which is preserved in the police Museum at New Scotland Yard, is the creation of an enterprising London journalist. I will only add that the second individual whom we suspected was caged in an asylum. The only person who had ever had a good view of the murderer at once identified him. But when he learned that the suspect was a fellow Jew, he declined to swear to him'.

There was an immediate reaction to Anderson's claims in this overtly racist interview, in the 'Jewish Chronicle' of the 4th of March 1910, when a Jewish journalist attacked Anderson for his blatantly racist views.

The journalist observed that his theory was nonsensical and that it condemned a whole neighbourhood of immigrants by tarring them with the same brush.

What proof did Robert Anderson have to support this view, the journalist asked? In fact, the article was nothing but a series of assertions and the only very detailed description of what the killer may have looked like in Anderson's careless and often less than grammatical prose, comes from an eyewitness statement made shortly after the last of the five so -called classic murders, ended with the murder of Jane Kelly in the September of 1888.

In the statements made to the police, the eyewitness has this intriguing description of the Ripper. The description comes from a document originating from a Metropolitan Police address in Commercial Street, and is dated the 12th of November, 1888.)

The description of the witness who saw the victim with a 'gentleman' describes the man in vivid and very clear detail.

'Age about 34, height about 5ft 6ins, complexion pale, dark eyes and eyelashes. Slight moustache cut off at each end and hair dark. Very surly looking, dressed in a long, dark coat, collar and cuffs trimmed and trim. The dark jacket under a light waistcoat, dark trousers, dark felt hat turned down in the middle. Button boots, decorated with white buttons; he wore a very thick gold chain, a white linen colour, a black tie with horseshoe pin and of respectable appearance.'

That is a report given by George Hutchinson, who was one of the detectives who gained access to the witness statement.

And now we shall look at further significant evidence.

The suggestion that the Ripper was of foreign extraction has been favoured by many people and this is supported by some of the phraseology used in the letters that the Ripper ostensibly sent, either to the Central Press Agency or to the police directly at various London police stations. However, let's first look at the Ripper's profile.

The very first offender profile of a murderer was commissioned by detectives of the Metropolitan Police about the personality of Jack the Ripper. Police surgeon Dr. Thomas Bond was asked to give his opinion on the extent of the murderer's surgical skill and knowledge.

Bond's assessment was based on his own examination of the most extensively mutilated victim; and, in addition, the post mortem notes from the four previous canonical murders in his reports to the police.

Following his detailed analysis of the body, or what might be better described as the dissected remains of the killer's last victim Mary Kelly, dated November 10, 1888, Dr. Bond mentions the sexual nature of the murders. He deduced that the feelings of hatred experienced by the murderer were coupled with elements of misogyny and rage.

Dr. Bond also attempted to reconstruct the murder, and interpret the behaviour pattern of the offender; soon thereafter, he came up with a profile or signature of the personality traits of the offender to assist the police investigation. The profile explained that five murders of seven which had occurred in a very small area of Whitechapel, had been committed by one person, a loner who was physically strong, composed, calm and daring.

This unknown offender would be quiet and harmless in his outward appearance; he said that in his opinion, the murderer was probably middle-aged, and 'neatly dressed'; also that the attacker most probably wore a cloak to hide the bloody effects of his attacks when he was out in the open and in retreat from the scene of the crime. He would be a loner, but without a solid occupation. He would be seen by those who knew or met him as eccentric, and he was very mentally unstable. He might possibly suffer from a condition called *satyriasis,* a sexual deviancy that is today referred to, as hypersexuality or promiscuity.

Dr.Bond also mentioned that he believed the offender had no specific anatomical knowledge and that he would not be able to confirm the oft- stated view, that he might have been a surgeon or a butcher. Bond's summary profile further explains:

'The murderer must have been a man of physical strength and great coolness and daring... subject to periodic attacks of homicidal and erotic mania.'

As a doctor in general medical practice, both in Birmingham and later as a GP in Southsea, it is entirely likely that Conan Doyle would have previously come across this condition, known in Victorian times, as Satyriasis. It is also very possible that he may have acquired a copy of the most famous autobiographical account of this condition, written by the enigmatic and anonymous gentleman and satyriatic sex-addict, 'Walter.'

In that century, 'satyriasis' was a condition only applicable to men and for which there was apparently no obvious cure, apart from frequent doses of bromide, or when this did not work, through barbaric practices such as penile cauterisation – a hideous remedy.

Conan Doyle himself had also written a detailed study of the symptoms of *tabes dorsalis,* a discreet account of the disease of syphilis, and he had even written a short story about it. This may be of great significance and it may have provided The Ripper with an additional motive for his vicious attacks on women.

Doyle also used the subject of syphilis as the theme for his story, 'The Third Generation.' In this now rarely anthologised tale, later reproduced in Doyle's 'Round The Red Lamp,' a young aristocrat visits his GP with a skin condition diagnosed as a 'strumous diathesis' – otherwise known as *scrofula then*. The name given to the condition by Doyle is merely a euphemism for syphilis.

The young man is told by his doctor in the tale that he must not even consider going through with his marriage, and, moreover, that he has been cursed by an hereditary illness. Several references are made to his ancestor's 'hereditary blight.' The afflicted visitor then makes this impassioned plea:

'"But where is the justice of it, doctor?" cried the young man, springing from his chair and pacing up and down the consulting-room. "If I were heir to my grandfather's sins as well as to their results, I could understand it, but I am of my father's type. I love all that is gentle and beautiful- music and poetry and art. The coarse and animal is abhorrent to me. Ask any of my friends and they would tell you that. And now that this vile, loathsome thing- ach, I am polluted to the marrow, soaked in abomination! And why? Haven't I a right to ask why? Did I do it? Was it my fault? Could I help being born? And look at me now, blighted and blasted, just as life was at its sweetest. Talk about the sins of the father - how about the sins of the Creator?" He shook his two clinched hands in the air - the poor impotent man with his pin-point of brain caught in the whirl of the infinite.'

During the period when Doyle was practising as a doctor, the 1870s, there was a relatively new view of human sexuality gaining ascendance. Several 'authorities' on the subject regarded male sexuality as an important biological imperative, a popular idea which added fuel to many Victorian writings on the male gender; but these assertions, in turn were countered by those who argued that 'civilisation' enabled humans to altogether transcend their purely animal instincts.

This view acquired a public voice through the 'Social Purity Campaign' which stood against what they viewed as the sexual 'double standard', and for the need for male as well as female continence outside of marriage. Though the female Purity campaigners were sometimes mocked as 'puritans' who had failed to attract a spouse, the movement certainly succeeded in raising public concern over brothels which, especially in the East End of London, had reached a record high at the time when the Ripper struck; there was a popular theory that the Ripper had contracted syphilis from a prostitute; this, in turn, was why he took his own form of barbaric vengeance on the women whom he perceived as 'whores' or 'drabs'. His decision to remove the uterus of one victim has been interpreted as a direct attack on the "essence of being a woman" – and experts believed he removed his victims' organs partly as trophies but also in order to mark his hatred of all womankind. I personally believe it to be convincing that Conan Doyle shared this view of the Ripper's profile. Yet the question I must pose is this: exactly why did he not make known publicly this analysis?

The sensational depiction of a Ripper murder, which appeared in 'The Police Gazette' in 1888.

THE RIVER THAMES

Illustration from the 1890 edition of 'The Sign of Four.'

One other thing about Jack's killing spree, which has attracted previously only scant notice, has been the possible use of the River Thames as a useful getaway route. In that period, the Thames was where poorer people got their drinking water from. However, it also acted as an important water-highway through the city.

In the novel by Charles Dickens 'Our Mutual Friend,' Jesse "Gaffer" Hexam – a waterman, and the father of Lizzie and Charley, makes a living by robbing corpses found in the river Thames.

In this classic novel, the great river and conduit, the Thames, is described in eloquent detail, lying in the midst of that vast overflow of London, where it is seen, not only as a huge and tainted sewer but also as a place of secrets, death and concealment. The two characters depicted in the opening of the story, Jesse "Gaffer" Hexam – a waterman and the daughter Lizzie, make a meagre and perilous living by robbing corpses found in the river Thames. His former partner, Rogue Riderhood, turns him in for the murder of John Harmon after Harmon's body is supposedly dragged from the river. A search is mounted to find and arrest Gaffer, but he is discovered dead in his boat.

For years, Gaffer has made his living as a waterman, retrieving corpses and taking the cash in their pockets, before handing them over to the authorities papers in the pockets of the drowned. In the novel, Dickens uses many images that relate to water. Phrases such as the "depths and shallows of Podsnappery," and the "time had come for flushing and flourishing this man down for good" are examples of such imagery. Some critics see this visual imagery as excessive, thus creating a feeling of caricature, but in the case of these descriptions of the river, this only serves to intensify the connection between the reader's fear of criminality and the sense of the Thames as a living but malign being, from whose waters, terrible secrets may soon be revealed. Thus, Dickens' account of the River

Thames carries within it that melancholy and disturbing Gothic horror of Poe, which so frequently imbues the work of Conan Doyle;

'Allied to the bottom of the river rather than the surface, by reason of the slime and ooze with which it was covered, and its sodden state, this boat and the two figures in it obviously were doing something that they often did and were seeking what they often sought. Half savage as the man showed, with no covering on his matted head, with his brown arms bare to between the elbow and the shoulder, with the loose knot of a looser kerchief lying low on his bare breast in a wilderness of beard and whisker, with such dress as he wore seeming to be made out of the mud that begrimed his boat, still there was a business-like usage in his steady gaze. So, with every lithe action of the girl, with every turn of her wrist, perhaps most of all with her look of dread or horror; they were things of usage.'

Here, Dickens portrays a dark, macabre London, inhabited by such disparate characters as Gaffer Hexam, a scavenger trading in rotting corpses; the enchanting but mercenary Bella Wilfer; the social climbing Veneerings; and the unscrupulous street-trader, Silas Wegg. The novel is richly symbolic in its vision of death and renewal in a city dominated by the fetid Thames, and the ever present corrupting power of money.

In the 1880s, the great River Thames would have been shrouded in virtual blackness at night, and anyone who either worked on the river or might have given a large tip to a lighterman, would have escaped arrest or even a cursory challenge by the Thames River Police.

The river police operated with both the Met. Police but also the City Police. The Thames River Police was formed in 1800 to tackle theft and looting from ships anchored in the Pool of London and in the lower reaches and docks of the Thames. It replaced the Marine Police, a police force established in 1798, by magistrate Patrick Colquhoun and justice of the peace John Harriott and had been part funded by the West India Committee to protect trade between the West Indies and London.

It is claimed that the Marine Police was England's first ever police force, but they had fewer numbers than the other divisions, having at their disposal several small, low bottom boats and only three steam launches.

Doyle favoured the idea of The Ripper using The Thames as a dark tunnel, where he could be entirely undetected and invisible from the riverbank, and this image is beautifully delineated in 'The Sign of Four,' where, in the penultimate chapter of this Holmes story, one of the murderers, Jonathan Small, is chased by a steam launch down to Gravesend where Small, who has a wooden leg, attempts an escape by launching himself from the boat straight into a bank of mud.

In my trilogy of books, 'The Criminal World of Sherlock Holmes,' I conjectured that it is certain that Jack the Ripper used the river, following his dastardly butcheries in Whitechapel. This is a highly likely scenario, since the consuming darkness of the river was legendary.

After dusk, an impenetrable gloom fell on its dark waters, thus enabling many criminals to escape without even a trace into the various parts of the city.

In the middle of the 19th century, Henry Mayhew and other social commentators were able to comment on the great number of robberies committed on the river Thames. These declarations differed in value, for example, from 'The little ragged child stealing a piece of rope or a few handfuls of coal from a barge,' to 'the lighterman carrying odd bails of silk, worth several hundred pounds.'

The Thames River Police, dragging a body from the river's dark waters. From 'The Strand Magazine.'

Looking to the long lines of shipping along each side of the river, these river criminals relied on the vessels that daily ploughed their way along its route. They were able to slip aboard the dense shipping in the docks and then emerge laden with untold wealth. And thus we should not be surprised at the level of almost unseen crime which flourished along the river's course.

The river had its own populace, some of whom belonged to, or depended on the criminal classes. The 'mudlarks,' so called, consisted of boys and girls who varied in age from eight to fourteen. These were, in their appearance, much like the Baker Street Irregulars. Many of them were described in Sherlock Holmes' time as 'coal light workers,' groups of mainly Irish youths, employed by older men, who were made to get coal from the ships illegally, which often their mothers would then take to the street and exchange for food. The children would get between the barges, lift up one end of the canvas and then knock the pieces of coal into their mouths, which they would then pick up afterwards at the dockside. They frequently sold these coals in and among the lower classes of people for a few halfpence each. When arrested by the Thames River Police, some of the Mudlarks obtained short-term spells of imprisonment, from three weeks to a month. But other, more repetitive offenders were sent to reformatories for two to three years.

Further up on the Thames from where Holmes and Watson entered the police steam launch, could be seen at low tide, groups of older women picking up coals in the bed of the river. One woman, described as 'a robust creature dressed in an old cotton gown with a straw bonnet tied round with a handkerchief', was often seen in the neighbourhood of Blackfriars Bridge, where there were small groups of ragged dressed females from 10 to 50 years. Some of them started their career with stealing rope or coal from barges, then proceeded to take the more valuable copper from vessels, and afterwards went down in the cabins and stole other goods.

There was even a class of boys who sailed the river in very ancient boats and often got on board into craft under the pretext of sweeping. They'd leave the barges laden with coffee, sugar or rice, stealing anything they could get their hands on. They were again described as 'ragged and wretched in appearance'.

These youths were expert swimmers, and ranged from 12 to 16, attired, or rather, dis-attired in a similar way to the other ragged boys in the metropolis, and in appearance, much like the Baker Irregulars. Some of them were healthy, some slept in barges and others inhabited some of the local lodging houses.

The level of unseen crime on the banks of and in the waters of the River Thames was notable, all of which gives, in my opinion, credence and support to the idea that the Ripper may also have had links to some of the criminal fraternity, who may have supported him either invisibly or unknowingly. There was a great degree of smuggling of contraband goods on the river by foreign seamen, upon their arrival from foreign ports, in the shape of tobacco, coal, handkerchiefs and jewellery.

Mayhew reports how, one morning, a policeman once spotted a group of chimney sweeps who had stolen merchandise from a boat and were leaving in a steam vessel, carrying with them some large bags. On searching the bags, he found several packages of manufactured tobacco. The chimney sweeps were arrested, and discovered to have in their possession £100 each. They were sentenced to six months each in prison, and having refused to pay their fines, were then imprisoned for an additional spell.

I had for long entertained the notion that the lightermen, who plied their craft and helped to convey people up and down the River Thames, may have had what was tantamount to a season ticket with Jack the Ripper, and if Conan Doyle's convincing theory that the perpetrator of these crimes may have been an American it would have been only too easy for a lighterman to convey him down river to Gravesend, from where boats headed across the Atlantic and beyond, even to the shores of the USA.

The reputation of the lightermen who plied their trade in these river taxis during that period was not above reproach. Mayhew, for example, quotes an account of two men who, in April 1858, were charged with robbery from barges at Wapping. They received quantities of dye, wire, and other commodities near the London Docks. Then they took the barge with the stolen property on board to

Rotherhithe, landing at the Elephant Stairs, where they were taken away in a cart.

The property was never recovered. But the two men were sentenced to 18 months at the Criminal Central Court.

Mayhew comments that many of the lightermen were often 'dissipated in their habits, and then resorted to thieving when they lacked money.' They spent time dancing, in the concert rooms on the notorious Ratcliffe Highway, a place also mentioned by Holmes. They generally were known to cohabit with prostitutes and they were 'an entirely different class of men'. He compares them to the River pirates, who also lived with prostitutes, but who were generally smarter and better dressed.

In case anyone thinks that Mayhew's descriptions are exaggerated, my own family history has a light to shed upon the matter of the reputation of the lightermen.

When, at the end of the 19th century, my great uncle was found dead, his stiffened body stretched out on top of steps leading down into the river, in the region of Greenwich, it was discovered that he had been robbed of his takings as a newsagent. And because there were no witnesses to the crime, the perpetrator of this vicious murder was never discovered. Hence, the reputation that the Thames acted as a cloak of invisibility, under which crimes often could be committed, was a view which was shared by many Londoners of that time, including my grandfather Frederick Morrison, the murdered man's younger brother.

CONAN DOYLE AND CRIMINOLOGY

'He is the Napoleon of crime, Watson...'

According to Adrian Conan Doyle, the author's son, in a letter sent to Tom Cullen, a researcher, Adrian had this to say about his father's views regarding Jack The Ripper:

"I do remember that he considered it likely that the man (the Ripper) had a rough knowledge of surgery and probably clothed himself as a woman to approach his victims without arousing suspicion on their part."

As was proved several times in the George Edalji case,[1] Doyle understood much about psychological profiling and how it worked; unlike some members of the Metropolitan Police, it must be admitted. He would therefore have both read and thoroughly comprehended what Hans Gross, the famous contemporary of Conan Doyle and his detective, what he had to say about this method of investigation, which, as we know, began with the first ever criminal profile, that of the Ripper himself.

In Gross's classic work about the motives of many murderers, 'Psychological Crime Investigation', the

---

[1] Edalji was an Indian immigrant, a parsee, who received several poison pen letters. He was later arrested on charges of horse maiming

Austrian ex-magistrate wrote this:

'If we stop with the phenomena of daily life and keep in mind the ever-cited fact that everybody recognises at a glance the old hunter, the retired officer, the actor, the aristocratic lady, etc., we may go still further: the more trained observers can recognise the merchant, the official, the butcher, the shoe-maker, the real tramp, the Greek, the sexual pervert, etc. Hence follows an important law -- that if a fact is once recognised correctly in its coarser form, then the possibility must be granted that it is correct in its subtler manifestations.'

A most Holmesian statement here, which might have had the sage of Baker Street himself nodding in agreement. Gross then goes on to explain:

'The boundary between what is coarse and what is not, may not be drawn at any particular point. It varies with the skill of the observer, with the character of the material before him, and with the excellence of his instruments, so that nobody can say where the possibility of progress in the matter ceases.

'When he speaks of stupid and intelligent faces, he is a physiognomist; he sees that there are intellectual foreheads and microcephalic ones, and is thus a craniologist; he observes the expression of fear and of joy, and so observes the principles of imitation; he contemplates a fine and elegant hand in contrast with a fat and mean hand, and therefore assents to the effectiveness of chirognomy; he finds one hand-writing scholarly and fluid, another heavy, ornate and unpleasant; so he is dealing with the first principles of graphology;--all these observations and inferences are nowhere denied, and nobody can say where their attainable boundaries lie.'

So did Doyle study the handwriting of the Ripper and know the name of the Ripper? I think he did, but he was not going to disclose it. We can be certain, however, that, among the papers and books sold which formed that great collection of criminological works owned by Doyle, but auctioned after the writer's death, there might have been some clue into the final revelation of the man the world subsequently knew as 'Jack the Ripper.'

Is it at then possible, to demonstrate that Conan Doyle had quietly and discreetly worked out the identity of this enigmatic killer?

The period of murders under consideration extends initially from August 31st to November the ninth, 1888. During that time, five prostitutes were murdered in the East End of London. In my opinion, there was an additional murder which was the murder in Castle Alley near a railway arch. This murder, though denied as relevant by most Ripperologists, is perhaps worth considering as worthy of inclusion, and also since from the extensive reports in Doyle's copy of 'The Portsmouth Evening News', we might then deduce, by inference, that Doyle would have gathered much of his data from Press reports during this period. We might, like him, assume that the attacker wore female attire, and, as some of the detectives under the instructions of Commissioner Macnaghten speculated, this case bore the signs of an interrupted attack by a man disguised as a woman.

Prior to the 'railway arch' murder, however, the so-called 'canonical' Whitechapel murder victims were as follows:

Mary Ann Nichols, who was killed at Buck's Row in Whitechapel. on August the 31st. Then, Annie Chapman, also a person who was suspected of earning money from immoral earnings, was killed in Hanbury Street, on September the eighth in that same year.

Next was a woman called Elizabeth Stride, who died on September the 30th at Berners St., Catherine Eddowes, who died at Mitre Square.

Lastly, on September 30 of the same year, Mary Jane Kelly, who was gruesomely slaughtered at a place called Miller's court on November the ninth, 1888.

A look at the murders prior to the railway arch murder reveals that each of the victims had their heads almost completely severed and also this kind of detail was reported in the newspaper, which Doyle would certainly have read when he was a GP in Southsea.

In addition to these details, in five of the cases, the woman's abdomens were gouged, or opened.

The very last murder was reported in an unusually

graphic depth and detail in the Portsmouth Evening News. Throughout this affair, no one at The Yard seems to have taken much consideration of the totality of information in the news reports. However, this totality of factual detail provides a very detailed profile of the murderer and an obvious series of links, which we can then comprehend, and trace in a forensic chain.

Conan Doyle first visited Scotland Yard's Black Museum, on December the second, 1892, four years after the Whitechapel Ripper murders. He would already have scrutinised the reports given by the attending surgeons who investigated the state of the bodies and who also later gave talks to the Crime Club members.

And here now is something which, up to this moment, has never been considered in any depth.

Conan Doyle would be interested in the *perversity* of the crimes, especially in connection with the knowledge that he had acquired from his reading of the forensic analysis of psychotic behaviour, which he would have read about, not only in Krafft Ebing's classic study *Psychopathia Sexualis* but also in the work of the Austrian judge, and renowned Austrian criminologist, Hans Gross.

I believe that Conan Doyle then used his literary skills and his formidable imagination to come to a well-informed view of the possible identity of the Ripper.

WOMEN AS VICTIMS

'To Sherlock Holmes, she is always '*the* woman,'

– Dr Watson.

The women of the Sherlock Holmes Saga are not infrequently described to the reader in piteous and oppressed terms, rather like the victims of the Ripper. They are often, also like those women, seen as victims of exploitation by predatory males. They range from Beryl Stapleton, who is corrupted and led to a conspiracy with her husband to kill Charles Baskerville, to Violet Smith who is forced against her will into an illegal marriage, (The Solitary Cyclist); a woman framed for murder by her employer's wife, ('Thor Bridge'); a wife whose lover has no option but to beat her husband to death rather than to witness her being savagely beaten, (The Abbey Grange,); a daughter locked permanently in a room rather than submit to her odious father's marital designs upon her, (The Copper Beeches); and lastly, a woman who is drowned with her lover and has one of her ears cut off , which is then sent by post to her sister (The Cardboard Box).

As William Booth wrote, in his polemical essay, which attempted to wag the finger at politicians and the failures of social reform in the Victorian age:

'We talk about the brutalities of the dark ages, and we profess to shudder, as we read in books of the shameful exaction of the rights of feudal superior. And yet here, beneath our very eyes, in our theatres, in our restaurants, and in many other places, unspeakable though it be but to name it, the same hideous abuse flourishes, unchecked. A young penniless girl, if she was pretty, is often hunted from pillar to post by her employers, confronted always by the alternative - Starve or Sin. And when once the poor girl has consented to buy the right to earn her living by the sacrifice of her virtue, then she is treated as a slave and an outcast by the very men who have ruined her. Her word becomes unbelievable, her life an ignominy, and she is swept downward ever downward, into the bottomless perdition of prostitution.

The Holmes story of Miss Kitty Winter, for instance, and her vengeful vitriol throwing attack on the prosperous businessman and Austrian voyeur, in the tale of 'The Illustrious Client' is all the more poignant, when you consider the age in which this story was being created. For though it was published in March 1923, the story is actually set earlier, in the September of 1902.

THE RIPPER'S LOATHING OF 'FALLEN WOMEN'

'It is not the cold which makes me shiver, Mr Holmes. It is fear.'

- Helen Stonor in 'The Speckled Band.'

London, particularly sections of it, like the Ratcliffe Highway in the east but also Shadwell, Spitafields, and Whitechapel - were greatly affected by the trade of prostitution, and I have no doubt that Kitty Winter, in desperation, and plagued by poverty, found herself in need of a solution by becoming a prostitute.

There were different types of prostitutes. And, judging by the drawing which accompanied the 'Strand Magazine' story of 'The Illustrious Client,' poor Kitty was not one of the more wealthy ones.

Prostitution in London, particularly in those areas commented on in the many books dealing with Jack the Ripper, was literally sectioned up into types of prostitutes. There were very few districts of London that didn't boast one variety or another of these women. They counted among their customers the commercial traveller, who'd come to town on business, which is highly likely in the case of Jack the Ripper, to have included the commercial traveller; the middle - class gentleman and the tradesmen, and the scores of artisans and manual and factory workers who had come to London for a spending spree, or a change of scenery.

The client would find most certainly what he sought in the Haymarket or Windmill Street, and the surrounding areas. The choice of prostitute was extremely varied and child prostitution was rampant as Oscar Wilde discovered, initially to his pleasure, but subsequently, to his inevitable and personal cost.

In fact, ironically, the chances of a man being mugged in that area were at their very lowest, compared to areas such as the West End which catered for the more high - class 'lady of the night' and because a wealthier person would present a possible means of employment for a whole night. In the 1880s, a number of the popular night houses and casinos in areas such as Cremorne gardens and the Argyle Rooms were devoted to drink and dance, activities which inevitably attracted the work of the prostitutes. And the women who were obliged to ply their trade went to the music halls.

I have already mentioned, one of the most notorious areas of all was the Ratcliffe Highway in London in the East End. At the time when Sherlock Holmes began his career in Baker Street, this street ran parallel with the river from Whitechapel to Stepney. And so it was very well placed to serve the huge collection of docks on either side of the Pool of London.

In every street, in every public house, and in every lodging house here, were a huge number of brothels, which used to be populated with visiting sailors of all nations. And they were all looking for the same thing. When William Acton wrote about the prostitutes of London, he visited a place in the 1880s and went to a prostitutes' lodging house, which had eight rooms.

Each of these rooms had been set at two shillings a night. And the landlady informed him that they were each hired more than twice for sexual congress in the course of an evening.

The anonymously, lust - inspired 'Walter', who wrote extensively about prostitution in London in his erotic six volume sexual odyssey book, 'Walter'[2] visited these places, when he frequently made expeditions to slum areas, in order to find prostitutes that he could afford, since he had fallen on hard times at that time of his life. And so he had to resort to wearing his oldest clothes, masking his face with the peak of a large cap, in order that he would not be recognised by those who might have seen him elsewhere.

---

[2] 'My Secret Life', the anonymous and highly erotic memoirs of a Victorian English gentleman called Walter. This work which I republished in 6 volumes in 2019, under the title, 'Satyriasis,' is a paean to a life devoted to the tireless pursuit of the carnal. As Walter's sexual and moral behaviour is revealed, we are left with indelibly bizarre insights into life behind the closed doors of Victorian society. Walter was thought to have been the alias of a wealthy collector of erotica, Edward Ashbee, but that theory is by no means justified or indeed provable, as I demonstrated in my introductions to the work.

He would have been an obvious target, being a man with money in his pocket, and wearing a gold chain, clearly visible to passers-by, connected to an expensive gold watch.

And of course such places were also swarming with a great number of beggars. At that time when Holmes' underworld agents roamed these mean streets they would soon be seen pleading for pennies in the same breath as they confided obscenities, in the hope of perhaps enlisting a potential client for buggery or oral sex acts in the back streets.

For in the slum areas of all large towns in Britain at that time, there were simply hundreds of displaced young, truant children who had to live by their wits, and had to do so by begging and stealing, and often prostituting themselves.

Of course, campaigners like Ashton blamed a prostitute and her plight on the shoulders of men. But each then would explain or justify it by referring to the principle of supply and demand.

But were any of the Rippers victims actually prostitutes? The historian, Dr Hallie Rubenhold argues that 'sexist' views of police officers and researchers over the past 130 years have inaccurately portrayed them.

In her book – 'The Five' [3]– she shows at least three women victims held jobs such as laundry maids and servants.

Acton claimed the vice of women who were street walkers, (yet another Victorian euphemism for the term 'prostitute,' the most haunting of which I would say, was 'drab'), was fuelled by a number of factors, amongst which was 'natural sinfulness'.

The preference to be idle, he argued, rather than to work hard to obtain a living, he claimed, did not entirely derive from a state of extreme poverty. He believed that the desire to be a prostitute might be influenced even by genetic factors. In fact, he was not wrong in some of his less extreme conclusions.

A letter written to the Times newspaper in 1858, by a prostitute, claimed that the thousands of women who were compelled to take to prostitution were poor women toiling on starvation wages, and, if they were simply to allow misery and famine to repress them they would have to 'render up your body or die'.

In the late Victorian age when Holmes and Watson witnessed the burning of Gruner's face, there were literally hundreds of women who swelled the ranks of prostitutes, who ranked among their number former dressmakers or hat makers, shoe binders or shop workers. All these people

---

[3] 'The Five,' by Haille Rubenhold, Penguin Books,

suffered as a result of the economic deprivation of the period.

Recent historians – especially feminist writers – have correctly seen the plight of the solitary woman in working class Victorian Britain, as a vulnerable female with limited options, turned sacrificial victim. This is a viewpoint I must entirely agree with. In a seminal review of one such historian of criminology, BSC, Volume 22, Issue 5, Paul Bleakley writes:

'Judith R. Walkowitz (1980) has written extensively on sex work in Victorian London and notes that the legal repression of prostitution (both streetwalking and brothels) in the late nineteenth century 'would directly affect the structure of the market for prostitution as well as the character of the women's relationship with the labouring-poor community.' In Walkowitz's view, sex workers in the period turned to prostitution as a way to free themselves from 'an oppressive work regime . . . [but] they were still operating within the narrow constraints imposed on them by a class-stratified and patriarchal society encouraged by this approach.' Later, he goes on to demonstrate the limited historical viewpoint thus cultivated:

'In the rush to use the Ripper story as a cypher for theoretical narratives, however, the basic facts of the case – that the Ripper was a killer of vulnerable women – is often forgotten, seen as secondary to his or her mythologisation as the 'perfect' killer.'

MURDER AND BLOODY MAYHEM

'There's a scarlet thread running through this business...'

– Sherlock Holmes.

Conan Doyle's bloody revenge tale, 'A Study in Scarlet', would be the first of many of these tales, bringing fame and prosperity to its young and ambitious writer, featuring a central protagonist detective with the unlikely name of Sherlock Holmes. As the years followed, these tales would eventually establish 'Sherlock Holmes' as a household word.

Now, over 150 years after his first appearance between the pages of the modestly produced 'Mrs. Beeton's Christmas Annual,' Holmes has been allowed into that rare Parnassus of public domain characters, like Sir John Falstaff, Count Dracula and, perhaps, more pertinently, Dr. Jekyll; and not forgetting the elusive and enigmatic master of disguise, the man the world still can never forget: Jack the Ripper, the Scarlet Pimpernel, not of crime fiction, but of true-life Victorian crime.

When one examines in detail (and there is a lot of detail in the Scotland Yard reports kept by the police surgeons of the time; each man being eminent, like meticulous Dr Bond, in his field of forensic expertise), the obsession with acts of mutilation, deliberate and calculated acts of sexual sadism and humiliation, is everywhere evident in the Whitechapel murders and to a degree that is almost sickening and overpowering.

The shocked demeanour of the police on entering the claustrophobic confines of the room in Miller's Court and being the first to witness there that awful scene of the dissected body, gives us the immediate impression that the Ripper was unique in the nature of the crimes achieved.

THE REAL JACK THE RIPPER

'You see, Watson, but you do not observe.'

– Sherlock Holmes.

By now I was beginning to see a definitive profile of Jack the Ripper. And the picture I was getting certainly supported most of Conan Doyle's suspicions, as confirmed in that interview with readers of 'Tit-Bits' magazine in 1894.

But why, I asked myself, did Doyle say nothing more and when, many years later, he provided a series of real-life famous crime articles for the Strand Magazine, did he not include his previously stated theories about the mystery of The Ripper?

In the next part of this examination I will list the reasons for the crime writer's apparent reluctance to provide the proof of this man's identity, a proof that I am certain, he shared and was privy to by Sir James Macnaghten, the assistant Commissioner for the Met. Police, who took on his role at Scotland Yard shortly after the last of the 'canonical' Ripper cases were investigated in 1888. This commissioner was not only in possession of prima facie evidence about his chief subject but that, like Conan Doyle, Doyle's friend in The Crime Club, the writer and ex-military man, Major Arthur Griffiths, was influential in the British Freemasons.

So, perhaps not coincidentally was Conan Doyle and, more significantly, the leading Ripper subject himself. It may also be of interest for readers to know that not only was Prince Albert a freemason but also was Edward VII's son, Albert Eddy Victor, the Duke of Clarence, who himself has been the subject of a detailed Jack the Ripper investigation.[4]

While Freemasonry is not itself a religion, all its members believe in a Supreme Being, or "Grand Architect of the Universe." Members come from many faiths, but one denomination in particular bars any crossover. The Catholic Church first condemned Freemasonry in 1738, prompted by concern over Masonic temples and the secret rituals performed within them. In the 19th century, the Vatican even called the Masons "the Synagogue of Satan." In contemporary times, the relationship between policemen and freemasonry has been heavily criticised. Wider afield, a recent update by www.ancestry.org revealed recently the social reformer Thomas Barnardo, famous bridge builder Thomas Telford, Rudyard Kipling, a great friend of Conan Doyle. Thousands of engineers, including Isambard Kingdom Brunel, who made Britain a world industrial power, were all members of lodges, as was also, key member, Lord Kitchener, Secretary of State at the

---

[4] 'Clarence,' by Michael Harrison. See bibliography.

start of World War One. Both Edward VIII, George VI, the Metropolitan Police Commissioner, Sir Charles Warren; these were also Masons, along with Warren's "eyes and ears" on the Ripper case, Detective Chief Inspector Donald Swanson. Not only this but also Coroners Wynne Baxter and Henry Crawford, who ruled at inquests on the Whitechapel murders, were Masons, along with at least three police doctors who examined the victims' bodies.

In addition to this, author Bruce Robinson, film director of 'Withnail and I', has claimed, in a recent book, that the Ripper murders bore the hallmarks of a Masonic ritual. He said proof came to him in the form of a pair of compasses carved into the face of victim Catherine Eddowes, the removal of meal buttons and coins from the bodies of Eddowes and Annie Chapman; and the cryptic graffiti daubed on a wall which was "the most flagrant clue of all". Robinson - whose book is called 'They All Love Jack: Busting the Ripper' claimed that "The whole of the ruling class was Masonic, from the heir to the throne down. It was part of being in the club'.

The freemasons had a huge influence over a controversial inquiry into the Titanic disaster in which more than 1,500 passengers and crew died. The secret archive showed that the judge who presided over the British Wreck Commissioner's inquiry was a Freemason, along with leading investigators and some people who completely escaped censure.

In the more recent past, there have been occasions

when masonic lodges have acted as nests of corruption for police; where detectives have rubbed shoulders with professional criminals in an atmosphere of friendship and loyalty, with disastrous results. When Scotland Yard's Obscene Publications Squad was destroyed by scandal in the late 1960s, twelve officers were jailed for taking bribes from pornographers. All of them were masons, including the head of the squad, Detective Chief Superintendent Bill Moody, who had even helped one of the pornographers he was supposed to be arresting to become a member of his own lodge.

For this sort of information about the Ripper to be publicly revealed, if Scotland Yard in 1889 had announced their suspect's name, there would have followed severe repercussions among many senior politicians of the time, including the monarch himself, who was, among masons, a highly respected senior lodge Freemason.

And further to these factors, my investigation of the barrister Montague Druitt does not stop here. For when Conan Doyle learned the truth about the man that he had known well and often played against in Surrey, where the Ripper lived and whose cricket club and town he frequently visited in Kingston, Surrey, Conan Doyle took the decision to resign his membership as a freemason, as a precautionary measure.

He was by now a celebrity author and had a reputation to consider, and if the reading public discovered that The Ripper had been a freemason, he would not wish this to be revealed. In fact, as this following chronology shows, throughout his career, Conan Doyle showed a marked ambivalence towards this strange and protective secret society:

26.01.1887: Arthur Conan Doyle was initiated into Freemasonry under the auspices of the Phoenix Lodge, No. 257, 110 High Street, Southsea, Portsmouth, at the age of 27. His sponsors were Mr. W. D. King (a former mayor) and John Brickwood (a brewer).

1889: He resigned from the Phoenix Lodge No. 257. This date corresponds with the discovery of the identity of the Ripper.

05.04.1900 : During the Boer War in South Africa, he attended a meeting at a scratch lodge: Rising Star Lodge No. 1022, at Bloemfontein with Bro. Rudyard Kipling.

23.03.1901: He accepted an honorary membership in the Lodge of Edinburgh No. 1 (St. Mary's Chapel, 96 George Street) in commemoration of his return to England.

1902: He rejoined the Phoenix Lodge No. 257

25.01.1905: He accepted an honorary membership to the Lodge Canongate Kilwinning No. 2 (Edinburgh).

1911: He resigned from the Phoenix Lodge No. 257 for the

second time without having progressed beyond the third degree in the Craft.[5]

But it was not only the subject's residence in Surrey and his membership of The Freemasons which troubled Conan Doyle. He was also troubled by the fact that he had played cricket against this man's cricket team for Surrey, in at least three matches in the summer seasons, prior to

---

[5] Major Wood, for years Doyle's secretary, was also a prominent freemason. Here is his obituary, dated 22 April. 1941. Note, by the way, the references to the MCC: 'By the death of Major Alfred Herbert Wood, M.A., which occurred suddenly on Saturday, Portsmouth has lost a prominent freemason, sportsman, and keen supporter of charitable work. He was 75 and a bachelor. Major Wood, member of an old Portsmouth family, was educated at Portsmouth Grammar School and in his last year there, had the unusual experience of being Hon. Secretary to the Church Congress which met at Portsmouth. Winning an open scholarship to Brasenose College, Oxford, he took his M.A. degree, and re-turned to Portsmouth as a master at the Grammar School. He was a close friend of the late Sir Arthur Conan Doyle (then practising as an oculist at Southsea) and later was for many years the famous novelist's private secretary and business manager. He had played cricket for Hampshire and also on occasions for the Hampshire Hogs and Hampshire Rovers, and was a member of the M.C.C. He was formerly for 15 years President of Portsmouth Football Association. Throughout the Great War he served in the 5th Royal Sussex Regiment, mainly in France, reaching the rank of Major. Wood was initiated to the Phoenix Lodge of Freemasons (No. 257) in 1895 and became W.M. in 1904. At the time of his death he was Treasurer. He was also P.P.J.G.D. in the Provincial Grand Chapter of Hants and Isle of Wight, and was a member of the Authors' Club Lodge (No. 3456). In Royal Arch Masonry he was P.Z. of Friendship Chapter (No. 257) and P.P.G.S.N. in the Provincial Grand Chapter. He was also

the subject's mysterious and inexplicable death, in the Christmas of 1888, the very year of the last and most savage of the East End slaughter of unfortunate prostitutes, Mary Kelley, in Mitre Court.

And this was the man who he had shared many a convivial chat with at the Blackheath Cricket Club pavilion, a man, like himself, who was the object of abiding regard for as the captain of his Surrey team.

Following a meeting of The Crime Club, Conan Doyle had met and become great friends with ex-Major Arthur Griffiths and had, in fact stayed with Griffiths for four days at his country residence.

Arthur, who liked to be known as 'Major Arthur Griffiths' was a British military officer, prison administrator and author who published more than 60 books during his lifetime. He was also a military historian who wrote extensively about the wars of the 19th century, and had been for a while, also a military correspondent for 'The Times' newspaper.

Born in 1838, at Poona, India, as the second son of Lieut. Colonel John Griffiths of the 6th Royal Warwickshire regiment. Arthur Griffiths had graduated from King William's College on the Isle of Man. Griffiths joined the British Army as an ensign in the 63rd Regiment of Foot on 13 February 1855. Serving in the Crimean War, Griffiths had participated in the siege of Sebastopol and had also fought during the capture of Kinbum, receiving the British Crimea medal for his valiant efforts. Doyle admired the man and, I believe, based his fictional creation of 'Colonel Sebastien Moran', the would-be assassin of Sherlock Holmes, in 'The Adventure of The Empty House,' a military man he had so much in common with.

Griffiths' later accounts in his well-respected books, 'Mysteries of Police and Crime,' had been described by one critic as 'sensational and grotesque', and 'designed to appeal to the baser fascinations' of his Victorian readers.

Yet the three volume edition, with its elegant green cloth binding, carried a wide selection of essays; not only about British but also European and North American crime and criminology, and its reputation was further endorsed by a special police edition aimed at senior detectives at Scotland Yard, which carried within that deluxe edition, full page photos of the Yard's senior detectives and commissioners of police. The success of this edition led Griffiths to write some 60 books, many of them mystery crime novels, such as 'A Son of Mars' and 'Fast and Loose'.

When the major entertained Conan Doyle for that four-day summer break, the esteemed criminologist, who knew personally not only the Commissioner but also many of the senior detectives who had been assigned to the Ripper case, most of them freemasons, he then learned the truth about the Yard's suspicions regarding the three most likely suspects of the Whitechapel murders; and Doyle probably listened in astonishment as the old war veteran explained the facts about Druitt to him.

As the recipient of the 'official view,' Griffiths published this key document in volume one of his 'Mysteries of Police And Crime,' in 1899, the year after the cessation of the murders, the same year that the commissioner decided to wind down the Ripper hunt and the very same year Doyle resigned from his Lodge. Griffiths wrote:

'The outside public may think that the identity of that later miscreant, "Jack the Ripper," was never revealed. So far as absolute knowledge goes, this is undoubtedly true.

'But the police, after the last murder, had brought their investigations to the point of strongly suspecting several persons, all of them known to be homicidal lunatics, and against three of these they held very plausible and reasonable grounds of suspicion. Concerning two of them, the case was weak, although it was based on certain suggestive facts.

'One was a Polish Jew, a known lunatic, who was at large in the district of Whitechapel at the time of the murder, and who, having developed homicidal tendencies, was afterwards confined in an asylum. This man was said to resemble the murderer by the one person who got a glimpse of him—the police-constable in Mitre Court.

'The second possible criminal was a Russian doctor, also insane, who had been a convict in both England and

Siberia.

'This man was in the habit of carrying about surgical knives and instruments in his pockets; his antecedents were of the very worst, and at the time of the Whitechapel murders he was in hiding, or, at least, his whereabouts was never exactly known.

'The third person was of the same type, but the suspicion in his case was stronger, and there was every reason to believe that his own friends entertained grave doubts about him. He also was a doctor in the prime of life, was believed to be insane or on the borderland of insanity, and he disappeared immediately after the last murder, that in Miller's Court, on the 9th of November, 1888.

'On the last day of that year, seven weeks later, his body was found floating in the Thames, and was said to have been in the water a month.

'The theory in this case was that after his last exploit, which was the most fiendish of all, his brain entirely gave way, and he became furiously insane and committed suicide.

It is at least a strong presumption that "Jack the Ripper" died or was put under restraint after the Miller's Court affair, which ended this series of crimes.

'It would be interesting to know whether in this third case the man was left-handed or ambidextrous, both suggestions having been advanced by medical experts after viewing the victims. It is true that other doctors disagreed on this point.

Sir Charles Warren, Commissioner for the Met, who was forced to resign over the Ripper case, was a leading Freemason.

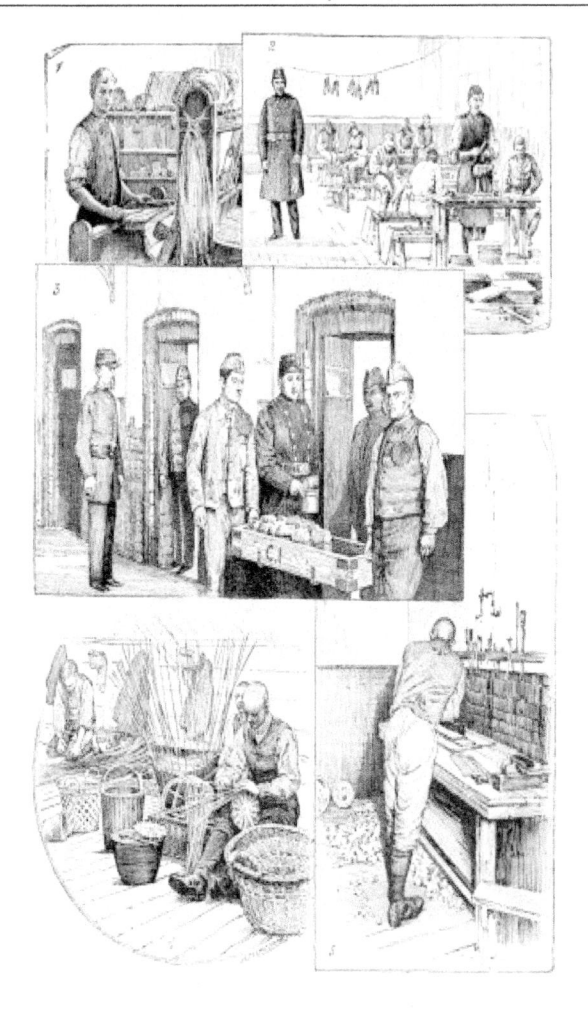

The Criminal Law Amendment Act made 'gross indecency' a criminal act subject to a prison sentence of two years. Druitt may have feared this possibility, if found guilty of molesting a pupil and the fear of enduring a prison existence as pictured may have caused his suicide.

'Yet the incontestable fact remains, unsatisfactory and disquieting, that many murder mysteries have baffled all inquiry, and that the long list of undiscovered crimes is continually receiving mysterious additions. An erroneous impression, however, prevails that such failures are more common in Great Britain than elsewhere. No doubt the British police are greatly handicapped by the law's limitations, which in England always act in protecting the accused. But with all their advantages, the power to make arrests on suspicion, to interrogate the accused parties and force on self-incrimination, the Continental police meet with many rebuffs'.

PLAY UP AND PLAY THE GAME

(Eton Boating Song)

Conan Doyle had been a keen cricketer all his life, (and continued to play until 1912, ever since he had been taught by the Jesuits at Stonyhurst College (1873-1875) and he knew how to play the game; later in his literary career, he was privileged enough to bowl out the famous living legend of late Victorian cricket, W. G. Grace. Doyle was possessed of a strong right arm and he was taller than the average cricketer, being over six feet. Doyle continued to play until 1912. He played in 440 matches, and for more than 50 different teams.

The main opposition teams were: Portsmouth (49 matches between 1884-1890), Hampshire Rovers (26 matches between 1890-1907), Norwood (71 matches between 1891-1894) and Marylebone Cricket Club aka M.C.C. (96 matches between 1899-1912). He played 10 first-class matches between 1900 and 1907.

He also played with his friend and secretary Alfred H. Wood, with his brother-in-law and writer Ernest W. Hornung and with other writers like J. M. Barrie or P. G.

Wodehouse (in 'Authors and Allahakbarries' teams). [6]

To Doyle, the game of cricket was a sacred cow. It affirmed both its players as downright moral and trustworthy citizens of the 'great Empire'; but also was a reminder of the players' loyalty to that wider community.

His love of the game was profound and he believed it to be character building among the late Victorian adherents who played it. And not least among that tribe, were many of the writers of the period. In an article he published in the 'Flintshire Observer', in 1899, he explained, [7]

---

[6] The Wisden Cricketers' Almanack published the following ACD obituary:

'Sir Arthur Conan Doyle, MD (Edin), the well-known author, born at Edinburgh on May 22, 1859, died at Crowborough, Sussex, on July 7, aged 71. Although never a famous cricketer, he could hit hard and bowl slows with a puzzling flight. For M.C.C. v. Cambridgeshire at Lord's, in 1899, he took seven wickets for 61 runs, and on the same ground two years later carried out his bat for 32 against Leicestershire, who had Woodcock, Geeson and King to bowl for them. In the Times of October 27, 1915, he was the author of an article on The Greatest of Cricketers - An Appreciation of Dr Grace. It is said that Shacklock, the former Nottinghamshire player, inspired him with the Christian name of his famous character, Sherlock Holmes, and that of the latter's brother Mycroft was suggested by the Derbyshire cricketers.'

My thanks are due to the website, www.arthur.conan.doyle.encyclopedia.org, for supplying this information.

[7] (2 November 1899, p. 6).

"... it was only in times of national excitement, such as we were now experiencing, that we found the true value of the love for games which ran in our veins. We were the one free country of Europe, and it was our duty to keep ourselves fit, as we were compelled to do so. Talk about calling out the reserves," he continued, "why, they had only commenced to call them out; the real reserves were the lovers of sport, the yachtsman, the rider to hounds, the cricketer, the football player — in a word, you all. If England were in a hole, we should have to trust to our sporting men to pull her out. The State had thought it right, to attend to the mind of the child, and they had only got to extend the principle by looking after the physical welfare of the country if they wished to keep the nation at the head."

The theory here espoused by the now celebrity author, and soon to be knighted Dr Doyle, would not have been so widely supported had the public come to know in the newspapers that The Ripper was an accomplished cricketer like himself; that they had played often together and that he too had learned the game at public school. Therefore, when he did find out the truth about this man, Doyle, understandably, kept the solution a secret.

Conan Doyle's appreciation of the cricketing legend, W, G. Grace, whose wicket he demolished at a charity match, Doyle using his strong, right arm spin technique.

THE CHIEF SUSPECT: THE FACTS OF THE CASE

(For much of the information that follows, I am indebted to the author, Christopher J. Morley, of the E-book, 'Jack the Ripper: A Suspect Guide' (2005).

Bearing in mind Sherlock Holmes' warning that 'there is nothing more deceptive than an obvious fact about the man who might fit the frame for The Ripper, we shall proceed.

Montague James Druitt was born at Westfield, Wimborne, Dorset, on 15 August 1857, the second son of seven children, to William and Ann Druitt. His father William was a doctor, as was his brother Robert and his nephew Lionel. Montague was educated at Winchester, and New College, Oxford where he graduated in 1880 with a third-class honours degree in the classics. While at Winchester he became heavily involved in the debating society, choosing political topics for his speeches.

That same year, he took up a teaching post at a boys' boarding school at 9 Eliot Place, Blackheath, run by Mr George Valentine.

In 1882, he started a second career in law and was admitted to the Inner Temple on 17 May. On 29 April 1885, he was called to the bar, and rented chambers at 9 King's

Bench Walk. The law list records him as a special pleader for the Western Circuit and Hampshire, Portsmouth and Southampton Assizes.

Druitt is often described as a failed barrister; if this claim were true, he would have been asked to vacate his chambers. He was successful until 1885, when things started to go wrong in his life.

First, his father died, at the age of 65, from a heart attack on 27 September 1885. Then his mother began to show signs of mental instability and became suicidal and delusional. She would later attempt to take her own life with an overdose of Laudanum. She was admitted to the Brook asylum in Clapton, London, where she remained until 31 May 1890, when she was sent to the Manor House asylum, Chiswick. She died there from a heart attack on 15 December 1890.

Suicidal urges appeared to be a trait in Ann Druitt's family. Her sister had also spent some time in an asylum after attempting suicide, and their mother committed suicide while insane.

On, or about, the 30 November 1888, Montague John Druitt was dismissed from his teaching job at the school, for what the press described as, 'serious trouble', but what exactly this serious trouble was, is unknown, but has led to speculation that it was due to a homosexual act with one of the pupils.

While there is no evidence to support this, it does

remain a possibility. Druitt was considered a successful handsome man, yet there is no record of any female companions during his life.

Druitt was last seen alive on 3 December 1888. When his eldest brother William, learned that Montague had not been seen for over a week and had been dismissed from his teaching job, he went to investigate, and found a suicide note amongst his brother's possessions which read, 'Since Friday I felt I was going to be like mother, and the best thing for me was to die'.

Montague John Druitt's body was fished out of the Thames, around 1:00pm, on Monday 31 December 1888, by Henry Winslade, a waterman. The body was believed to have been in the water for about one month. The body, which was fully dressed and bore no injuries, was brought ashore and searched by P.C. George Moulson, who found four large stones in the pocket of his overcoat, £2 and 17 shillings two pence in coinage, two cheques, one for £50, and one for £16, a first class season rail ticket from Blackheath to London, a second half return Hammersmith to Charing Cross, dated 1 December, a pair of kid gloves, a white handkerchief and a silver watch with a gold chain.

The inquest was held at the Lamp Tap, Chiswick before Dr Thomas Diplock. It was concluded that Druitt had committed suicide whilst of unsound mind. He was subsequently buried in Wimborne Cemetery on 3 January 1889.

Of course, none of the above cumulative evidence necessarily proves that Druitt was The Ripper.

However, as we shall soon see, when circumstantial evidence can be observed as a wide series of correlations, we are then left to the conclusion that:

'When you have eliminated the impossible, whatever remains, however improbable, must be the truth.'

That is another of the sayings of Conan Doyle's immortal creation, Sherlock Holmes.

FURTHER FACTS REGARDING DRUITT AND BLACKHEATH

If Druitt was The Ripper, then he most probably drank in The Princess of Wales, the pub right next to the Blackheath railway station (he was in the hockey team that was based there), and he would have walked up and down the hill to catch trains from Blackheath station to Charing Cross. From here he could also connect swiftly and easily with Whitechapel by rail or quite inconspicuously, by hansom cab.

At Blackheath he would have been spoiled for choice regarding which train to catch to Charing Cross, for trains arrived at 16 and 18 minute intervals because the station at Blackheath had the luxury of serving passenger trains supplied by the London, Brighton and South Coast Line and trains of the South Eastern Line.

Whitechapel station itself was originally opened in 1876 when the East London Railway (ELR, now the East London Line) was extended north from Wapping to Liverpool Street station. The ELR owned the tracks and stations but did not operate trains. From the beginning, various railway companies provided services through Whitechapel including the London, Brighton and South Coast Railway (LB&SCR), the London, Chatham and Dover

Railway (LC&DR), Great Eastern Railway (GER) and the South Eastern Railway (SER).

Blackheath village, c. 1880. Note the prominence of hansom cabs, a means of conveyance which would have speedily enabled Druitt to access the railway station.

The boys' prep school where in 1880, Druitt taught in Blackheath, 9 Eliot Place decided to embark upon a teaching career, is now residential, but then was home to several schools. Montague John Druitt's father died of a heart attack in 1885, and three years later, his mother committed suicide.

He was dismissed from the school for some "serious trouble", but for exactly what crime or moral misdemeanour, this remains a complete mystery, since it was not explained by his brother at the inquest which followed his death and neither did the headmaster of the boys; prep school wish to comment on it,

His body was found floating in the Thames at Chiswick on December 31st 1888

THE CRICKET LINK

Druitt was nominated for membership of the Morden Cricket Club in 1883 and elected on May 26 of the next year. His subscriptions (which were unenviable) were nevertheless paid in full at the time of his death. Druitt was later appointed treasurer and honorary secretary of the Blackheath Cricket, Gottball and Lawn Tennis Company in 1885. His address was then given as 9 Eliot Place, Blackheath.

Where exactly where was this man's 'digs'? Of this we cannot be certain, but it is certain that from the rail station they would have been in easy striding reach of the station or he could have taken one of Mr Tilling's speedy cabs from the nearby cab rank which was adjacent both to the station and the pub.

One of the police reports implied that there was additional evidence against him that could not be brought to light, and that he was "sexually insane", which was a Victorian euphemism for homosexuality. In his autobiographical book, 'Memories And Adventures,' for example, Doyle reflects on the harsh treatment in the media of Oscar Wilde, following his incarceration and two-year prison sentence, when he found to be guilty of 'acts of gross indecency,' adding that, though he admired

Wilde's literary achievements, he considered his behaviour as a type of illness/

There is a far better account of the discovery of Druitt's body from the inquest, including this rather grim list of items discovered with his body:

Four large stones in each pocket

£2.17s.2d cash

A cheque for £50 and another for £16

Silver watch on a gold chain with a

spade guinea as a seal

Pair of kid gloves

White handkerchief

First-class half-season rail ticket from Blackheath to London

Second-half return ticket from Hammersmith to Charing

Cross dated December 1, 1888

What did happen at 9 Eliot Place?

My intrigue in Druitt as a possible subject rose with the publication of two books in the 80s and 90s – at which point, incidentally, some of the children who attended the school surely would have still been alive and it would have been useful to hear their side of the story regarding the barrister.

Was this man the unfortunate victim of a period incapable of understanding a school teacher with homosexual proclivities, or did the deaths of his parents finally push Druitt into a psychotic state towards murder? I can't help wondering if there might be a yellowing scrap of paper tucked away somewhere in Blackheath that might shine a light upon the business.

WHAT WE DO KNOW ABOUT MONTAGUE DRUITT

Montague John Druitt; he was a graduate of Winchester College and an avid sportsman who was discovered drowned in the bank of the Thames on December 31, 1888. He was considered by many, including several senior Yard detectives, to be the number one suspect in the case. Interestingly though, there is very little evidence primary or forensic evidence with which to implicate his guilt.

Druitt was the second son of a medical practitioner, William Druitt, born August 15, 1857 in Wimborne, Dorset.

Researcher Peter Birchwood, in his superb profile,[8] sums up the facts about the mysterious barrister and allows us, most usefully, a glimpse into Druitt's family from his careful researches into the 1881 census:

Dwelling: Westfield House

Census Place: Wimborne Minster,

Dorset, England

Source: FHL Film 1341505 PRO Ref RG11

---

[8] Peter Birchwood: see acknowledgements page.

Piece 2093 Folio 13 Page 19

William DRUITT M 60 M Wimborne,

Dorset, England

Rel: Head

Occ: F.R.C.S.Not Practising

Anne DRUITT M 51 F Shapwick,

Dorset, England

Rel: Wife

Georgiana E. DRUITT U 25 F Wimborne,

Dorset, England

Rel: Daughter

Edith DRUITT 13 F Wimborne,

Dorset, England

Rel: Daughter

Occ: Scholar

Ethel M. DRUITT 10 F Wimborne,

Dorset, England

Rel: Daughter

Occ: Scholar

Ann FLIPP U 35 F Spetisbury,

Dorset, England

Rel: Servant

Occ: Cook

Edith DENNETT U 25 F Wimborne,

Dorset, England

Rel: Servant

Occ: Parlour Maid

Sophia E; 23 F Gosport,

Hampshire, England

Rel: Servant

Occ: House Maid

Educated at Winchester and New College, Oxford, Druitt was later to graduate with a third class honours degree in the classics in 1880 (Sugden).

While at Winchester, however, Druitt was heavily involved in the debating society, choosing mostly political topics for his speeches. He was known to denounce the Liberal Party as well as Bismark's influence as "morally and socially a curse to the world." His last speech contended that while previous generations believed 'man is made for

States,' it is a 'vast improvement that States should be made for man, as they are now.'

A sportsman as well as a speaker, Druitt was given a spot in the Winchester First Eleven (cricket) in 1876, and he was a member of the Kingston Park and Dorset Country Cricket Club. As noted in Brian Pugh's 'Chronology of the Life of Arthur Conan Doyle, the author visited the Kingston Park Cricket Club where he undoubtedly would have met and played matches against Druitt's team.

Druitt, like Conan Doyle, was noted to have had formidable strength in his arms and wrists, despite his appearance in the photographs of him which have survived. He also became quite expert and highly proficient at Fives, and won the Double and Single Fives titles at Winchester and Oxford.

On March 9, 1875, he achieved third position in a cricket ball throwing event at Winchester, with a toss of over ninety-two yards. Conan Doyle achieved similar success and was known among cricketers for his early spin technique, which he employed against W.G. Grace.

Immediately after graduation, Druitt began his teaching post at a boys' boarding school in Blackheath. In 1881, Druitt was introduced into the local membership of the Blackheath Hockey Club and later began to play for the Morden Cricket Club of Blackheath.

The next year, in 1882, Druitt again decided to focus

on a law career, and he was admitted into the Inner Temple on May 17. On April 29, 1885, he was called to the Bar. The Law List of 1886 places him both in the Western Circuit and the Winchester Sessions. Druitt continued to excel at the sport of cricket. He was nominated for membership of the Morden Cricket Club in 1883 and elected on May 26 of the 1884. His subscriptions (which were unenviable) were nevertheless paid in full at the time of his death. Druitt was later appointed treasurer and honorary secretary of the Blackheath Cricket, Gottball and Lawn Tennis Company in 1885. His address was then given as 9 Eliot Place, Blackheath.

In 1887 he is recorded as a special pleader for the Western Circuit and Hampshire, Portsmouth and Southampton Assizes (noted by Sugden – see bibliography).

In 1885, his father died from a sudden heart attack. Although his estate came to a total of £16,579 inheritance, the father left Montague and his two older brothers only a small proportion. In July of 1888, Druitt's mother Ann (nee Harvey) developed a form of dementia and having been certified insane, was sent to the Brook Asylum in Clapton. Yet through this vexing time, it appears that there were no notable effects of the grief felt by her son.

It seemed that to all outward appearances Druitt seemed to have been able to deal with the loss of both his parents within the small space of three years. However, this was clearly not the case since in the late November of

1888 Druitt must have committed suicide and subsequently he was found on Monday, December 31, 1888 floating near a mudbank in Chiswick in the Thames river.

Henry Winslade, a waterman working off Thorneycroft's Wharf in the river Thames, discovered Druitt's decomposed body around 1:00 PM that day, and after he dragged it ashore he informed the River Police. Constable George Moulston 216T made a complete listing of possessions found on the yet unidentified remains.

According to brother William's testimony (he had identified the corpse), Druitt was dismissed from his post at Blackheath School for an unknown reason (some authors have taken to suggesting that Druitt was dismissed for his homosexual tendencies, which perhaps caused him to make love to one of his students, and since the boys slept in communal dorms, this would have been observed by other pupils).

The date of his dismissal remains to this day ambiguous, as can be seen in the only known report to survive of the inquest testimony, here transcribed below from the 'Acton, Chiswick, and Turnham Green Gazette of January 5, 1889':

'William H. Druitt said he lived at Bournemouth, and that he was a solicitor. The deceased was his brother, who was 31 last birthday. He was a barrister-at-law, and an assistant master in a school at Blackheath. He had stayed with witness at Bournemouth for a night towards the end of October. Witness heard from a friend on the 11th of December that deceased had not been heard of at his chambers for more than a week. Witness then went to London to make inquiries, and at Blackheath he found that deceased had got into serious trouble at the school, and had been dismissed. That was on the 30th of December.

'Witness had deceased's things searched where he resided, and found a paper addressed to him (produced). The Coroner read the letter, which was to this effect: - "Since Friday I felt I was going to be like mother, and the best thing for me was to die." Witness, continuing, said deceased had never made any attempt on his life before. His mother became insane in July last. He had no other relative'.

As Sugden[9] points out, the date given here of December 30th is erroneous. As points out in his e-book, 'The wording alone makes it possible that it was in reference to either William's inquiries or Druitt's dismissal. If it was in reference to the former, it is doubtful that William would wait nineteen days after receiving word that his brother was missing to inquire into his whereabouts at Blackheath School. If it referred to the latter, however, it is impossibly incorrect, as Druitt was discovered the day after the 30th of December, and was estimated to have been in the water for upwards of three

---

[9] See bibliography.

weeks or more. Sugden concludes, with reasonable certainty, that December 30th is a misprint for November 30th, a date which makes much more sense.

Assuming it was November 30th on which occurred Druitt's dismissal, the few facts of the case fall nicely into place, assuming it was his dismissal which finally prompted his suicide. The 30th was a Friday, which hearkens back to his suicide note: 'Since Friday I felt I was going to be like mother, and the best thing for me was to die.' Also, remember that among his possessions were two cheques for £50 and £16, respectively. They may have been settlement cheques of Druitt's salary written upon his dismissal. Finally, there was also found an unused return ticket from Hammersmith to Charing Cross dated December 1'.[10]

The question thus arises: when did Druitt actually commit suicide? His tombstone has the date as December 4th, and this in turn is most likely to have been originated from William's inquest testimony that "on the 11th of December [the] deceased had not been heard of at his chambers for more than a week." Yet, as Mr Morley notes,[11] the use of the word more — this suggests a date before the 4th of December. Sugden places the date as December 1st, the day after his dismissal.

---

[10] Morley.
[11] Ibid.

As Morley concludes,[12] 'This paints a picture of a successful barrister, suddenly overwrought by his dismissal at his second job in Blackheath. He accepts his two settlement cheques from his former employer and sulks home, thoughts of suicide entering into his mind. The next morning he writes his note, walks to the Thames with four stones in each pocket, perhaps glances at his cheques one last time, and throws himself into the icy water. It all seems to make sense.

Everything, except for motive, that is. Druitt was still a successful barrister, and the school position was only a secondary means of earning money. He was rather high and well-known in the social status, and could easily have found another job if need be. So why the suicide?'

One thing is certain. If, as I now believe, Druitt had interfered with one of the pupils or perhaps had developed an attachment to a pupil and then been rebuffed, he would certainly also have been aware of the Criminal Law Amendment Act 1885, commonly known as the Labouchere Amendment, made "gross indecency" a crime in the United Kingdom. In practice, the law was used broadly to prosecute male homosexuals where actual sodomy (meaning, in this context, anal intercourse) could not be proven.

The penalty of life imprisonment for sodomy (until

---

[12] Ibid.

1861 it had been death) was also so harsh that successful prosecutions were rare. The new law was much more enforceable. It was also meant to raise the age of consent for heterosexual intercourse. Section 11 was repealed and re-enacted by section 13 of the Sexual Offences Act 1956, which in turn was repealed by the Sexual Offences Act 1967, which partially decriminalised male homosexual behaviour.

Most famously, Oscar Wilde was convicted under section 11 and sentenced to two years' hard labour, and in the 20th century, Alan Turing was convicted under it and sentenced to oestrogen injections (chemical castration) as an alternative to prison.

More plausible, however, was that Druitt's mind was slowly deteriorating. The death of his father in 1885, and the committal of his mother only six months before his death could very well have played a heavy part in the matter. Furthermore, mental illness seems to have run in the Druitt family.

Ann Druitt, his mother, was later to die in the Manor House Asylum in Chiswick in 1890, having suffered from depression and paranoid delusions. Morley notes:[13] 'She once attempted suicide by overdosing on laudanum. Her mother before her had committed suicide, and her sister had tried to kill herself as well. Montague's oldest sister

---

[13] Ibid.

killed herself in old age by jumping from an attic window'.

And so it must stand — suicidal tendencies ran in the Druitt family, and it most probably was an overreaction at his dismissal, which prompted him to follow suit. Regardless, the inquest was held Wednesday, January 2, 1889, before Dr. Thomas Diplock at the Lamp Tap, Chiswick. It was concluded that Druitt committed suicide 'whilst of unsound mind.' Unfortunately, the coroner's papers no longer exist.

And so the story of Montague John Druitt ends, and his alleged involvement in the Whitechapel Murders begins.

The brunt of the argument contending that Druitt was the Ripper lies with a quote made by Inspector Macnaghten in his famous memoranda, who was referring to Montague in the following quote:

'I have always held strong opinions regarding him, and the more I think the matter over, the stronger do these opinions become. The truth, however, will never be known, and did indeed, at one time lie at the bottom of the Thames, if my conjectures be correct!'

As the author points out, the description of this suspect differs slightly in Macnaghten's memoranda and Scotland Yard's public record files. The former reads:

Mr. M.J. Druitt a doctor of about 41 years of age & of fairly good family, who disappeared at the time of the

Miller's Court murder, and whose body was found floating in the Thames on 31st Dec: i.e. 7 weeks after the said murder. The body was said to have been in the water for a month, or more; on it was found a season ticket between Blackheath & London. From private information I have little doubt that his own family suspected this man of being the Whitechapel murderer; it was alleged that he was sexually insane.

The Scotland Yard file reads:

A Mr M. J. Druitt, said to be a doctor & of good family, who disappeared at the time of the Miller's Court murder, & whose body (which was said to have been upwards of a month in the water) was found in the Thames on 31st December - or about 7 weeks after that murder. He was sexually insane and from private information I have little doubt but that his own family believed him to have been the murderer.

Primary or forensic evidence which supports Druitt's being the Ripper is all but non-existent. In fact, his only true link can be made in his appearance and his likeness to many witness accounts.

All but one witness gave estimate of age close to Druitt's (31): P.C. Smith (28), Israel Schwartz (30), Joseph Lawende (30), and George Hutchinson (34-35). Elizabeth Long gave an age of forty, but she admitted she did not see the suspect's face.

As for appearance, three major witnesses report the

Ripper as having a moustache (which Druitt had), although the colour varies from "dark," to "brown," to "fair." Druitt was also of respectable appearance, always known to have been well-dressed. All witnesses except for Lawende (who said the suspect had the appearance of a sailor) support this possibility: Long described a man of 'shabby genteel,' Smith and Schwartz both labelled the man as respectable, and Hutchinson went so far as to describe him as "prosperous-looking."

In terms of build, however, Druitt falls short. He was a slender man, while witnesses described the man as being from medium to heavy build, stout, and broad shouldered. Almost unfailingly, the suspect was labelled consistently as "foreign-looking" and "a Jew."

Other problems arise. It is generally accepted that the Ripper was an inhabitant of the East End (Sugden)[14], but Druitt had little or no experience in or around the area of Whitechapel. He was living at 9 Eliot Place, Blackheath during the murders. But could that address have been used as a "base" for the murders?

Sugden[15] cites contemporary train schedules in order to disprove this theory. According to him, there was no all-night train service between London and Blackheath. The last train leaving Blackheath in 1888 left at 12:25 AM and the earliest leaving London for Blackheath was at 5:10

---

[14] See bibliography.
[15] Philip Sugden, historian of Jack the Ripper.

AM.

Although for the Nichols (3:40 AM), Chapman (5:30 AM) and Kelly (4:00 AM) murders the Ripper may have been able to jaunt over to the station and take a train back to Blackheath with very little time wasted waiting for the first train to arrive, this does not hold true for Stride (1:00 AM), Eddowes (1:44 AM) or Tabram (2:30 AM). If the Ripper had killed them and needed to take a train back to Blackheath, Sugden claims, he would have to remain in the area for "perilous hours" just asking to be detected. Still, he admits, the killer could have remained in a common lodging house for some time, although a respectable man such as Druitt in such a place would seem suspicious.

Tom Cullen, author of and noted Druittist,[16] argues that Druitt's known chambers at 9 King's Bench Walk could have been used, as they are within walking distance of the East End. Yet Sugden again refutes this, citing the Ripper's known movements on the night of the double murder. King's Bench Walk was west of Mitre Square (site of the second murder), and yet the killer is known to have gone north east directly after killing Eddowes and dropped her apron in Goulston Street. Would the killer have risked detection by entering the lion's den northward if he had indeed planned to find refuge to the west?

---

[16] 'The Crimes and Times of Jack the Ripper,' Tom A. Cullen Bodley Head, 1965

One of the most often quoted sources of evidence against Druitt, however, is his documented cricket schedule during the murders. On Friday and Saturday, August 3 and 4, Druitt was in Dean Park, Bournemouth. He was there again on August 10 and 11 playing the Gentlemen of Dorset. Tabram was killed on Tuesday, August 7. Would it not make sense that Druitt would have stayed in the region of Bournemouth if he was playing two consecutive weekends? Druitt was known to have played for Canford, Dorset, against Wimborne at Canford on September 1st, the day after Nichols' murder. On September 8th (day of Chapman's murder) Druitt played at 11:30 AM against the Brothers Christopherson on the Rectory Field at Blackheath.

This provides no real conclusive evidence against Druitt, but it does seem unlikely that he could have killed Chapman at 5:30 AM, and still had time to catch a train to Blackheath, remove his bloodied clothes, was up, ate breakfast, and was on the field by 11:30, especially considering that he would probably have been prowling the streets the entire night before.

And so, Mr Morley concludes, goes the arguments of those who believe Druitt could *not* have been the Ripper. However, what I would like to know is this: why would Macnaghten have made such a seemingly groundless claim? Some contend it was because he was horrendously under-informed of the case, and perhaps based his theory on mere memory.

When Macnaghten says in the memorandum, *"from private information I have little doubt but that his own family believed him to have been the murderer,"* one must look closely at the diction of that statement. We have no clues as to who the informant was whom Macnaghten refers to, but from the way he words his statement, it would seem as if it would have been a Druitt family member.

And yet if one of Druitt's relations had informed Macnaghten that they believed he may have been the Ripper, would Macnaghten not rather have said he has evidence that Druitt's family believe him to be insane? This leads one to believe that perhaps Macnaghten was basing his claims on hearsay and rumour, rather than actual private information he himself received. It's a great puzzle.

Another statement made by Macnaghten was that the Ripper's brain, "after his awful glut on this occasion (Kelly's murder), gave way altogether and he committed suicide; otherwise, the murders would not have ceased."

And yet there is still, to this day, no evidence which shows that serial killers cannot simply stop killing. According to Sugden, "more recent experience ... seems to demonstrate the contrary."

There are, of course, and we must not forget this aspect of the case, other reasons besides suicide which could have prevented the Ripper from continuing his crimes after Kelly, such as incarceration (in prison or an asylum), emigration, accidental or natural death, or even a bout of illness.

Even more damning is the statement that "despite the dramatic increase of such crimes in recent decades, no major offender is known to have committed suicide. (Sugden)"

What's fairly incomprehensible are the many errors in Macnaghten's notes, regarding Druitt. The commissioner states that Druitt lived with his family, but records show that *he lived alone at 9 Eliot Place.* He stated that Druitt had committed suicide around the 10th of November, *three weeks before it actually occurred.* He also stated that Druitt was about 41 at the time of his death, *overestimating by ten years.* Finally, he mentions Druitt as being a doctor, *when he was a barrister and schoolmaster.*

Still, Macnaghten was intelligent, having been part of a team combatting terrorism, and it is doubtful he would have placed such merit in a suspect without due cause. Perhaps more evidence or documents will be found eventually one day in the future, which would shed some light on Macnaghten's motives for choosing Druitt as chief suspect in The Ripper Cae.

Detective Abberline, the most rigorous of all the detectives who investigated the Ripper, didn't acknowledge the fact, as others such as Anderson have so famously done, that the Ripper was known to have been dead soon after the autumn of 1888. In his interview with the 'Pall Mall Gazette' in 1903, he says:

'You can state most emphatically that Scotland Yard is really no wiser on the subject than it was fifteen years ago. It is simple nonsense to talk of the police having proof that the man is dead. I am, and always have been, in the closest touch with Scotland Yard, and it would have been next to impossible for me not to have known all about it. Besides, the authorities would have been only too glad to make an end of such a mystery, if only for their own credit.

And so remains the case of Druitt. His acceptance as a Ripper suspect must lie in the belief that Macnaghten had more information than he wanted others to know — information which he claims he destroyed so as not to cause an uproar.

One must also admit that Druitt would have found it difficult, but not, in my opinion, impossible to commit the murders in time to return to his cricket games, especially in the cases of Nichols and Chapman.

And here is where I believe that several past Ripperologists have overlooked a distinct possibility that Druitt may have, as Conan Doyle hinted, in that interview given in 1894, that Druitt was a great deal brighter than they had perhaps imagined. As a cricketer, we know he was strong enough to strangle his victims. He enjoyed a respectable middle class professional profile as a barrister and school teacher. Just like Conan Doyle, he was respected in the sporting communities which he participated in. He had access to public and private transport and frequently made use of these facilities. But we have forgotten one extra factor: the close proximity of Whitechapel to the Thames,

Here, in the dark environs of the ancient, stinking great river of the metropolis, we find Druitt's essential retreat. The subway under the River Thames, that is, the original tunnel was completed by February 1870, and a press launch was held the following April. The underground railway opened for public use on 2 August, charging 2d for first class and 1d for second class, first class ticket holders merely having priority for the lifts and when boarding However, the system was unreliable and uneconomic.

The company went into receivership in November 1870, and the railway closed on 7 December 1870, four months after opening/

The railcar and steam engines were removed, gaslights installed and the passenger lifts replaced with spiral staircases. The tunnel was then reopened to pedestrians on 24 December 1870 at a toll of ½d and became a popular way to cross the river, averaging 20,000 people a week (one million a year). Its main users were described as "the working classes who were formerly entirely dependent on the ferries." The railcar and steam engines were removed, gaslights installed and the passenger lifts replaced with spiral staircases.

The Italian writer Edmondo De Amicis (1846–1908) gave a description of a passage through the subway in his Jottings about London.

'As I was thinking of these things I disappeared from the world indeed, going down a lighted spiral staircase which buries itself in the earth on the right bank of the Thames, opposite the Tower. I went down and down between two dingy walls until I found myself at the round opening of the gigantic iron tube, which seems to undulate like a great intestine in the enormous belly of the river.

The new improved tunnel shown here in 1870.

The inside of this tube presents the appearance of a subterranean corridor, of which the end is invisible. It is lighted by a row of lights as far as you can see, which shed a veiled light, like sepulchral lamps; the atmosphere is foggy; you go along considerable stretches without meeting a soul; the walls sweat like those of an aqueduct; the floor moves under your feet like the deck of a vessel; the steps and voices of the people coming the other way give forth a cavernous sound, and are heard before you see the people, and they at a distance seem like great shadows; there is, in short, a sort of something mysterious, which without alarming causes in your heart a vague sense of disquiet. When then you have reached the middle and no longer see the end in either direction, and feel the silence of a catacomb, and know not how much farther you must go, and reflect that in the water beneath, in the obscure depths of the river, is where suicides meet death, and that over your head vessels are passing, and that if a crack should open in the wall, you would not even have the time to recommend your soul to God, in that moment how lovely seems the sun! I believe I had come a good part of a mile when I reached the opposite opening on the left bank of the Thames; I went up a staircase, the mate of the other, and came out in front of the Tower of London.

Finally, note this fact, dear reader.

In September 1888, the subway briefly achieved notoriety after a man with a knife was seen in the tunnel at the time when Jack the Ripper was committing murders in nearby Whitechapel.

Now consider this. The time taken to travel the pedestrian tunnel for a fit walker is 9-12 minutes. From here, the Ripper had a choice of no less than seven ferry boat stations to enable him to travel either upriver or down. If alighted at Woolwich, he could traverse Woolwich down the High Street, then make his way via back streets, to Greenwich Royal Park, then find himself on Blackheath itself, thus completely avoiding arrest on a train. The total travelling time for the venture would be approximately,:

Outbound journey

1, Eliot Place, across the heath, thence to rail station = 12 minutes,

2 Train from Blackheath to Charing Cross = 20mins.

3 Charing Cross to Whitechapel via underground, -= 15 mins, or in a cab.

Total outbound journey = 50 mins.

Allow an hour.

Murder itself = possibly 1 hr duration,

Return journey.

From (example) Mitre Court, Whitechapel, To River Thames wherry station = 30mins (this includes the Tower tunnel).

Down Thames to Woolwich by wherry = 40 mins

Woolwich wherry station, walk through Woolwich to Eliot Place = 30 mins.

Total journey time = 1hr 35mins.

As the reader can see, the Ripper could successfully navigate his way to the murder scene, commit the murder and be back indoors in approximately just under 4 hours.

Seen from this analytical aspect, it would have been more than easy for the murderer to have completed his nocturnal tasks.

I must therefore conclude the following, based on cumulative circumstantial evidence:

1 The Ripper was certainly known to Doyle.

2 Doyle was unable to make any public assertion as to the identity of the man, partly because there was no direct, but only circumstantial evidence which no jury would have convicted him on.

3 Such forensic traces which were collected and examined from crime scenes would not have been admissible because of the lack of reliable blood analysis and fingerprinting techniques then available.

4. The eye witness evidence was of a conflicting nature and very fragmentary.

5. Some of the transcripts relating to the Druitt case and other Ripper cases was either lost by detectives or deliberately concealed and possibly destroyed by Robert Anderson.

M. Druitt. Probably taken on graduation day.

The Duke of Clarence, a Ripper suspect.

BIBLIOGRAPHY

Anderson, Robert: Criminals and Crime, 1907

The Lighter Side of My Official Life, 1910.

Begg, Paul (2003). Jack the Ripper: The Definitive History. London: Pearson Education.

Begg, Paul (2004). Jack the Ripper: The Facts. Barnes & Noble Books.

Bell, Neil R. A. (2016). Capturing Jack the Ripper: In the Boots of a Bobby in Victorian England. Stroud: Amberley Publishing.

Cook, Andrew (2009). Jack the Ripper. Stroud, Gloucestershire: Amberley Publishing.

Cornwell, Patricia (2002) Portrait of a Killer. London: Time Warner.

Costello, Peter, (2006), Conan Doyle, Detective. Robinson.

Cullen, Tom (1965) Autumn of Terror. London: The Bodley Head.

Curtis, Lewis Perry (2001). Jack The Ripper & The London Press. Yale University Press.

Eddleston, John J. (2002). Jack the Ripper: An Encyclopedia. London: Metro Books.

Evans, Stewart P.; Rumbelow, Donald (2006). Jack the Ripper: Scotland Yard Investigates. Stroud, Gloucestershire: Sutton Publishing.

Evans, Stewart P.; Skinner, Keith (2000). The Ultimate Jack the Ripper Sourcebook: An Illustrated Encyclopedia. London: Constable and Robinson.

Evans, Stewart P.; Skinner, Keith (2001). Jack the Ripper: Letters from Hell. Stroud, Gloucestershire: Sutton Publishing.

Fido, Martin (1987), The Crimes, Detection and Death of Jack the Ripper, London: Weidenfeld and Nicolson.

Gordon, R. Michael (2000). Alias Jack the Ripper: Beyond the Usual Whitechapel Suspects. North Carolina: McFarland Publishing.

Griffiths, Major Arthur (1899). Mysteries of Police and Crime, Vol 1. Gutenberg. Vols 2 -3 almost unobtainable.

Gross, Dr Hans, Criminal Investigation, Eng, edn., 1908. Online version on Gutenberg.

Harrison, Michael, Clarence: The Life of H.R.H. the Duke of Clarence and Avondale(1864-1892), Allen & Unwin, (1974).

Holmes, Ronald M.; Holmes, Stephen T. (2002). Profiling Violent Crimes: An Investigative Tool. Thousand Oaks, California: Sage Publications, Inc.

Honeycombe, Gordon (1982), The Murders of the

Black Museum: 1870–1970, London: Bloomsbury Books.

Hyde, H. Montgomery (1976) The Cleveland Street Scandal. London: W. H. Allen.

Jones, Kelvin I., The Criminal World of Sherlock Holmes, vols 1-2, MX Books, London, 2022.

Jones, Kelvin I., The Whole Art of Detection, Cunning Crime Books, 2019. Ten of the master detective's monograph on the art of detection, with introduction & useful appendices relating to Victorian crimes and criminals, edited by Kelvin I. Jones.

Jones, Kelvin I., (ed.) Satyriasis, Walter's 'My Secret Life', newly edited with introductions, in 6 volumes, Cunning Crime Books, 2019.

Krafft-Ebing, Richard, Leopold Von – Psychopathia Sexualis, new edition, Introduction by Kelvin I Jones, Cunning Crime Books, 2019.

Knight, Stephen (1976) Jack the Ripper: The Final Solution. London: Harrap.

Leighton, D. J. (2006), Ripper Suspect: The Secret Lives of Montague Druitt. Stroud, Gloucestershire: Sutton Publishing.

Leighton, D. J. (2004), Montague Druitt, Portrait of a Contender, Hydrangea Press.

Lynch, Terry; Davies, David (2008). Jack the Ripper: The Whitechapel Murderer. Hertfordshire: Wordsworth

Editions.

Christopher J. Morley, E-book, 'Jack the Ripper: A Suspect Guide' (2005).

Marriott, Trevor (2005). Jack the Ripper: The 21st Century Investigation. London: John Blake.

Meikle, Denis (2002). Jack the Ripper: The Murders and the Movies. Richmond, Surrey: Reynolds and Hearn Ltd.

Rivett, Miriam; Whitehead, Mark (2006). Jack the Ripper. Harpenden, Hertfordshire: Pocket Essentials.

Rumbelow, Donald (1990). Jack the Ripper. The Complete Casebook. New York City: Berkley Publishing Group.

Rumbelow, Donald (2004). The Complete Jack the Ripper. Fully Revised and Updated. London: Penguin Books.

Sugden, Philip (2002). The Complete History of Jack the Ripper. New York: Carroll & Graf Publishers.

Toughhill, Thomas (2008).The Ripper Code. The History Press Ltd.

Thurgood, Peter (2013). Abberline: The Man Who Hunted Jack the Ripper. Cheltenham: The History Press Ltd.

Waddell, Bill (1993). The Black Museum: New

Scotland Yard. London: Little, Brown and Company.

Werner, Alex (editor, 2008). Jack the Ripper and the East End. London: Chatto & Windus.

Whittington-Egan, Richard; Whittington-Egan, Molly (1992). The Murder Almanac. Glasgow: Neil Wilson Publishing.

Whittington-Egan, Richard (2013). Jack the Ripper: The Definitive Casebook. Stroud: Amberley Publishing.

Wilson, Colin; Odell, Robin; Gaute, J. H. H. (1988). Jack the Ripper: Summing up and Verdict. London: Corgi Publishing.

Woods, Paul; Baddeley, Gavin (2009). Saucy Jack: The Elusive Ripper. Hersham, Surrey: Ian Allan Publishing. Begg, Paul (2003) Jack the Ripper: The Definitive History. London: Pearson Education,

APPENDIX A:

THE TUNNEL MURDERS

Question: Did Druitt actually die as a result of drowning in the Thames? Or was the body that of the Duke of Clarence?

Globe - Wednesday 14 November 1888 RIPPER

SIGHTING NEAR TOWER TUNNEL

Some excitement was caused in the neighbourhood of the Westminster-Bridge-road, Lambeth, about half-past ten o'clock last night by cries of Jack the Ripper being raised. A man was seen loitering about in Tower-street in a rather suspicious manner, and carrying a shiny black bag, and but for the appearance a constable would have been roughly treated by the crowd. On being questioned, the man gave the name of Clayton. His bag having been searched by the constable, and found to contain nothing of a suspicious nature, the man was not further detained. He had the appearance of an American, with a dark moustache, and was wearing soft round hat and a tweed cape-coat.

Dublin Evening Telegraph - Tuesday 27 June 1893

A mysterious murder committed in Rotherhithe, in the South East of London — in the early hours of Sunday morning has attracted considerable attention from the fact that in many particulars it bears a striking similarity to the series of notorious murders attributed to Jack the Ripper. In the first place the district in its character is very similar to Whitechapel. Although on opposite sides of the Thames, both districts are adjacent to the river, and are inhabited by a class which ekes out a miserable existence by a number of occupations, various and precarious. Moreover, communication between Whitechapel and Rotherhithe is rapid and busy. The Thames tunnel supplies one means and the district railway another, so that if Jack 'the Ripper" contemplated business in Whitechapel on Sunday evening he could speedily shift the scene of operation to Rotherhithe if circumstances were not propitious in his usual haunt. Again, the victim of Sunday morning's tragedy belonged to that class which supplied all the "Ripper" victims. The manner in which the murder was committed also indicates a relation between it and the Whitechapel series.

On Sunday morning, the woman was found with her head nearly severed from her body, and most sensational circumstances; the wound was inflicted from right to left—a peculiarity which characterised all the "Ripper" murders. It must he added, however, that the remains were not mutilated, an omission on the "Ripper's" part explainable by the fact that persons were attracted to the scene by the dying shrieks of the victim, on which account the murderer thought it prudent not to complete his ghastly programme. The authorities evidently do not place the crime in the category of ordinary murders, as no less than twelve of the most experienced detectives in Scotland Yard are at present engaged in tracking the murderer, who is described as a short man with a sailor-like appearance.

APPENDIX B:

CONAN DOYLE, BLACKHEATH AND THE CEDARS

The Cedars, Lee, location of the Sherlock Holmes tale, 'The Man with the Twisted Lip.'

'YOU KNOW THAT PARTICULAR QUARTER'

"You know that particular quarter, the monotonous brick streets, the weary suburban highways. Right in the middle of them, a little island of ancient culture and comfort, lies this old home, surrounded by a high sun-baked wall mottled with lichens and topped with moss, the sort of wall - "

"Cut out the poetry, Watson," said Holmes severely. - "The Retired Colourman."

Not only was Conan Doyle most familiar with Blackheath and its environment; he also used the location for at least two of the Sherlock Holmes series. One of these featured the Cedars.

There were two occasions upon which Mr Sherlock Holmes was brought to Lee. One was in the June 1889, when he was called on to investigate the curious affair of the disappearance of Mr Neville St. Clair, and the other occasion concerned the investigation into the disappearance of the wife of Josiah Amberley, a retired "colourman" whose residence was at "The Haven" in Lcwisham.

Dr Watson, it will be remembered, was called out one evening by a friend of his wife, whose husband, Isa Whitney, was known to have been in an East End opium den called "The Bar of Gold". It was here also that Dr Watson met the disguised Holmes and the meeting led to the opening of the adventure later chronicled as "The Man with the Twisted Lip".

Holmes chose the hansom cab for his sojourn into this town of Kent (it is academic perhaps that in the previous year it had been transformed into the administrative county of London). If he had taken the train from Charing Cross, his journey would have been longer and more inconvenient. (Lee, Blackheath or Lewisham stations were available to him via the North Kent line. Borne on an extensive viaduct, the traveller passed through the suburbs proper - "squalid alleys and clamorous streets gradually giving place to large market gardens" as the S.E. Railway Guide put it.)

The "seven-mile drive" from Swan Lane to The Cedars would have cost five shillings in Holmes' day and the shortest route covered would be six and a half and not, as Holmes tells us, "seven miles". The journey, during which Holmes tells Watson, "We have touched on three English counties in our short drive, starting in Middlesex, passing over an angle of Surrey and ending in Kent" would start from Upper Thames Street and the "broad balustraded bridge" which they flew over would of course be London Bridge. From London Bridge they would continue down Southwark High Street, turning left along Great Dover Street, and coming out into the Old Kent Road. They would then carry on into New Cross Road. From here, they would turn right just after reaching New Cross Station into Lewisham Way.

Here Watson tells us "we had been whirling through the outskirts of the great town until the last straggling houses had been left behind, and we rattled along with a country hedge upon either side of us. Just as he (Holmes) finished, however, we drove through two scattered villages, where lights still glimmered in the windows."

The first of these two "scattered villages" can easily be identified as "Newtown" (no longer marked on modern maps), centered around Lewisham High Road; the cab would then come into the country once more with only a few scattered houses such as Llawrenn Villa and Stone House along the route. Then, after coming out of Loampit Vale, the cab would swing round into Lewisham Road, thus coming into the second village of Lewisham.

The cab here would turn left up Belmont Hill and the cab's destination, The Cedars, would be on its left. It is worth noting that The Cedars still stands today, and its outward appearance is still the same as it was in Holmes' day. All that has been altered is the inside of the building. A newspaper report of the 1920s tells us that "Messrs Hodson propose to commence almost immediately the development of 15 acres, forming part of the grounds of The Cedars. The mansion is, we understand, to be converted into flats. It is worthy of note that it is proposed to retain the outward appearance of "The Cedars", the only alterations contemplated being to the interior."

Watson describes "The Cedars" as "a large villa which stood within its own grounds." A description of The Cedars as it was in 1888 one year before Holmes' visit, still exists, and we are told that "The mansion is scarcely seen until we turn a belt of trees and find it close at hand: and the approach at once reveals the beauties to be seen beyond.

"In the front is a border of the finest collection of rhododendrons, with the clematis Virginian creeper and jasmine overhanging the windows in rustic form; and the venerable cedar of Lebanon, near the conservatory, at the top of the lawn . . ."

"Northward we look across the railway towards Blackheath at the head of the dell with the shrubberies at each side of the steep slopes which are dotted with trees; and include a fine plantation of the pinus Australasia and excelea of the Himalayas." That plant and many similar Himalayan species Holmes was no doubt to meet later, if we are to recognise his interest in botany. (Witness his words in "Wisteria Lodge"; "With a spud, a tin box, and an elementary book on botany, there are instructive days to be spent"). We are told by Holmes that "My room at The Cedars is a double bedded one". We also know that Holmes was "staying there while I conduct the inquiry". It will be remembered too that this was one of the cases that nearly foiled Sherlock Holmes, were it not for an all-night sitting in which he reached his solution "by sitting upon five pillows and consuming an ounce of shag".

The question has often been raised as to how Holmes reached his results, for there is no real explanation given at all. Mr Bernard Davies points out that part of the explanation may be that Holmes knew St. Clair through his acting days. But admirable as this deduction is it does not give us the answer to the question as to what gave Holmes the key to the problem. Mr Davies suggests quite correctly that "this was a case... of some chord of memory struck by chance as in "The Lions Mane." Now we know, and Holmes knew, that the name of the beggar suspected of murdering Neville St. Clair (and who was St. Clair in disguise as it turned out) was called Hugh Boone. This alias has its factual origins and although Holmes found that "it is always awkward doing business with an alias," the derivation of the name is easily discovered. A Boone family once lived at Lee "in an ancient red brick mansion, surrounded by a moat, in the Old Road, for many years called "Boone Mansion", and which was pulled down in 1824." However, the Boone family left a memorial behind them in the form of some thirty almshouses, built in 1826. These almshouses (no longer standing) faced Brandram Road, which leads into Belmont Hill, and which comes out almost opposite "The Cedars". Neville St. Clair would obviously have been aware of their existence as they were only a few hundred yards from "The Cedars", and it thus was quite natural that he should gain his alias from this source.

The proximity of these almshouses leads one to suspect that they also gave Holmes the clue to the true identity of "Hugh Boone". If he had seen the name, as is most likely, for he had been staying at "The Cedars", it may have well set off a train of thought in his mind which after the coaxing influence of the shag tobacco and the Eastern divan, produced that rare outburst of self-criticism: "I think, Watson, that you are now standing in the presence of one of the most absolute fools in Europe, I deserve to be kicked from here to Charing Cross."

The stationary type of begging practised by Neville St.

Clair was in fact much rarer than it is now generally supposed. Begging was illegal then, as it is now, and a person who drew a crowd round him in a busy thoroughfare was liable to attract the attention of a constable. The problem of begging in the capital had been partly created by the increased vigilance of the municipal police who drove the vagrants of the countryside into the metropolis. In the "paddingkins" or cheap lodging houses of the great city they could dodge the police much more efficiently and their anonymity served as an added protection. In the case of Hugh Boone, alias Neville St. Clair, he avoided prosecution by pretending "to a small trade in wax vestas". The competition was fierce and often vicious in those days. To succeed at begging, you not only had to contend with the police; you also had to hold your pitch against competitors.

The procedure of "standing a pad on a fakement" (this involved carrying a card round your neck detailing your claim to charity, tragic past history, etc.) was at the best, risky. The blind beggars (the genuine ones, that is) were best off. Gonorrhoea, for which there was no cure, and smallpox, rife among the lower classes, claimed many victims and the blind man with his dog became a familiar object of Victorian sentiment. Sham blindness was surprisingly uncommon, mainly because it did not often go undetected for very long. If the police didn't realise it, then your own kind soon would.

Boone faked a limp according to Holmes, but "in other

respects he appears to be a powerful and well nurtured man." Perhaps that was just as well, for he would have attracted little sympathy from his begging colleagues. But it was, of course his appearance which drew in the money.

The return journey to Bow Street at 4.25 the next morning after Holmes all-night vigil would take approximately the same route as before. However, the cab would turn into the New Kent Road this time, and thence to the Elephant & Castle, turning off onto the London Road. At St. Georges Circus they would then turn into the Waterloo Road and as Watson notes "passing down Waterloo Bridge Road we crossed over the river". Here, however, arises one of those peculiar anomalies of unintended Watsonian misdirection, for we are told that "dashing up Wellington Street (we) wheeled sharply to the right and found ourselves in Bow Street". Now Wellington Street passes straight into Bow Street itself, the police station being on the right-hand side opposite Covent Garden Opera House. What is unaccountable is that Watson should have thought that they turned right at the end of Wellington Street to arrive at Bow Street. All I can suggest is that the cab turned right into Martlett Court, down by the side of the police station, and that Watson, seeing the name of Wellington Street a few seconds before, assumed that by turning right they were presumably turning into Bow Street.

It was not until many years later that Holmes and Watson once again visited Lee. The Neville St. Clair case took place in 1889 and Watson did not mention the locality again (Except for a fleeting reference of the residence of Mr John Scott Eccles at "Popham House" Lee) until he chronicled the affair of "The Retired Colourman". Both Mr Gavin Brend and Mr W.S. Baring-Gould date this case as 1898. This is deduced from the information Holmes supplies: "Retired in 1896, Watson. Early in 1897, he married a woman twenty years younger than himself. And yet within two years he is as broken a creature as crawls beneath the sun." It is assumed that Amberley was a "broken" man within two years of his retirement, by both commentators. However, it is just as logical to suppose that he degenerated to this state within two years of his marriage. This would fix the date of the case as 1899.

The identity of "The Haven" is slightly more difficult to trace than that of "The Cedars". Watson tells us that after leaving Amberley's house, he "had driven to Blackheath Station". Later we are told by Holmes that "it is only a few hundred yards to the station (from Amberley's house)". The station referred to could either be Blackheath Station or Blackheath Hill Station, the latter being nearer the centre of Lewisham. One is tempted to pick Blackheath Hill Station at first, but the station mentioned is specifically "Blackheath Station". A further objection to Blackheath Station is that it is in the village of Blackheath itself, and as Lewisham is mentioned as Amberley's residence the station that Watson would have come from was, one presumes, Lewisham Junction. In fact, though, Blackheath Station is just on the parish boundary line between Blackheath and Lee and by the London Government Act of 1899, Lewisham and Lee were united, forming a metropolitan borough. Thus Amberley's house could still legitimately be referred to as being in "Lewisham".

By 1889, Lewisham had become a sprawling suburb with a population of 92,000 people. Unlike today, however, it was still largely dominated by the middle classes. Men like Josiah Amberley were typical of the residents of this expanding borough. The station itself stands on high ground, "the fields (rising) abruptly above it to the top of the hill, and . . . covered with villa residences and pleasant gardens. There are handsome and convenient district churches", remarks The Handbook of Kent . . . The "Grammar School", founded by the Rev Abraham Colfe, 1650 is on Dartmouth Hill, ...and is in... the hands of the Company of Leather-sellers. It is in the vicinity of the Grammar School that Amberley resided.

Belmont Hill, which was then a narrow and steep country lane (now a busy main road) formerly had only three buildings: "The Cedars", The Rectory and St Margaret's Church. At the Blackheath end of this hill, however, originally stood a house called "Belmont" which was built in 1830. This house would only have stood a few hundred yards away up the hill from Blackheath Station, and we can be tolerably certain that this is the site of the house to which Watson gave the obviously disguised name of "The Haven".

The whole of the area north of Blackheath Station comes within the parish of Blackheath and not Lee, so the general southerly direction to which the house would have lain is also correct. ("When you have excluded the impossible, whatever remains . . . must be the truth" - Holmes) Watson, being a habitual addict of the hansom cab, would have taken one from Blackheath Railway Station. We find in 'Butts Historical Guide to Lewisham, Lee, Blackheath & Eltham', 1878 the following information: "Cab stand - opposite Blackheath Railway Station for four carriages. T. Tilling owner. Stable yard adjoining with 15 other cabs". The close proximity of the cab stand would be yet one more good reason for Watson to go to Blackheath as opposed to Lewisham Station, for he could then indulge in his Victorian habit, while Holmes, whose efficient expediency is notorious, obviously found it an advantage to bundle the "writhing and fighting" Mr Amberley into a waiting cab which would then speedily conduct him to the custody of the police under Mackinnon, no doubt awaiting the arrival of their miserly guest at the station. There is also mentioned in the Guide a "pocket time book . . . published monthly, price one halfpenny". But no doubt Holmes was satisfied with his Bradshaw. Of even more interest, however, is the list of fare rates. In Holmes' day a twelve month first-class season ticket fare between London and Lewisham (and Holmes and Watson always travelled first-class) cost twelve pounds, which approximates to something like an eightpenny daily return fare.

The railways were not without their problems in those days. Blackheath 2, like Lewisham, was experiencing an expansion of population during the years of Dr Watson's visit and the pressure on the rail traffic grew in proportion. In 1877, the railway bridge had been widened to accommodate more trains. Lengths of sidings, stables for the railway companies' horses and coal yards for local merchants all helped to expand the area. By 1883, the Bexleyheath Railway Company was floated to build a line from Crayford to Lee via Bexleyheath, but the South Eastern Railway pushed them out. The new line was finally built between 1891 and 1895. In 1897, the station was considerably improved. Cast iron canopies were built over the platforms and the platform was widened. In the year following Watson's visit the station experienced a visit from no less an august personage than Queen Victoria.

As for "The Haven", the original building with its "high sun baked wall" as Watson described it, was demolished in 1907 and as there is an unfortunate lack of detailed description about the house in local contemporary guides and documents, it is indeed a shame that Watson was told to "cut out the poetry" just when his monologue was becoming interesting. However, it is of interest that this stood only about half a mile away from, and stood on the same road as "The Cedars". To Holmes at least, who knew this area, it probably brought back pleasant memories. Indeed, if he was as well acquainted with the area as evidence suggests, he no doubt knew Blackheath well and may, if we are right in assuming his eternal obsession with guides and directories of all kinds, have even had a copy of Bradshaw's 'Descriptive Railway Handbook of Great Britain and Ireland'. (We know, of course, that he had the standard Bradshaw). This gives us an interesting picture of Blackheath as Holmes must have seen it.

"(This heath) is now a favourite resort of the inhabitants of London who come in crowds during the holidays and summer season - donkey riding being a favourite amusement. The heath is exceedingly picturesque and commands several very fine views".

It is comforting to remember that since Holmes and Watson's day the heath is one of the very few landmarks that have survived the onslaught of time. But then, for the eager pilgrim, there is always "The Cedars" to visit!

APPENDIX C:

THE CLEVELAND STREET SCANDAL:
THE DUKE OF CLARENCE AND
HIS DOPPELGANGER

The 'Telegraph Boy Scandal,' of 1889, in which many prominent homosexuals were involved, points to the unrestricted abuse of young children who were left to roam the streets of Victorian London. For many years, the General Post Office in London had employed young men of under sixteen years of age to deliver telegrams to private individuals within the city and beyond into the suburbs of London.

In the July of the year 1889, a police constable was investigating a theft from the Central Telegraph Office and, during his investigation stumbled across the fact that one of the employees, a 15 year old Telegraph boy, called Charles Thomas Swanscow was found to have a large sum of money. For which he had no satisfactory explanation. When questioned closely, he said that he had obtained a sum of money by 'acting on behalf' of male clients in a house in Cleveland St at number 19 and, moreover, had earned quite a considerable sum of money amounting to 14 shillings. When asked precisely how he had obtained this sum, he explained and then confessed to the policeman, that he had earned this money as 'ill-gotten gains'. When questioned as to what that actually meant, he explained that he had been in attendance at a male brothel, which happened to be situated locally within the city. At number 19 Cleveland St another boy was found to have been working with him who was an older boy of 18 years, one Charles Henry Truelove. He had also been working for Hammond in the brothel there, when the police conducted their raid. The boys revealed to the officer that there were some 'very upper class looking people' who were attending the house in Cleveland Street. And some of those they suspected, they told police, were connected with the aristocracy, including a member of the Royal family.

The case was then handed over to Senior Scotland Yard detectives who raided the brothel where they then found that Hammond had narrowly escaped custody by being informed by another visitor and had subsequently sought refuge at his relative's house in Gravesend, Kent. Armed with this knowledge and also the knowledge that two other boys have been implicated in the business of the brothel the process of interrogation and the arrests were taken charge of by Inspector Fred Abberline of the New Scotland Yard team. He was one of the most successful police officers of his generation at the Yard.

However, by the time that Abberline and his team arrived at the brothel, Hammond had long gone and Abberline and his detectives were only able to arrest two other participants who had been on loan to the male homosexuals at the brothel. They were subsequently arrested. On the way to the police station, one of these called Newlove named Lord Arthur Somerset and Henry FitzRoy, Earl of Euston, as well as an army colonel by the name of Jervois, as visitors to Cleveland Street.

Lord Somerset had certainly been seen there and he was the head of the Prince of Wales's stables. And although he was subsequently interviewed at length by police, no further action was taken against him.

An arrest warrant was then issued in the name of George Veck, an acquaintance of Hammond's, who had pretended to be a clergyman. Veck had worked at the Telegraph Office and had been sacked for "improper conduct" with the messenger boys. A seventeen-year-old youth found in Veck's London lodgings told police that Veck had gone to Portsmouth. The police subsequently arrested Veck at Waterloo railway station.

On 16 December 1889, a new trial commenced in London, when Newlove's and Somerset's solicitor, Arthur Newton, was charged with obstruction of justice. It was claimed by the police that he conspired to prevent Hammond and the two boys from testifying by offering them passage and money to go and escape arrest and go abroad. Newton was then defended by Charles Russell, and the prosecutor was Sir Richard Webster, the Attorney General. Newton pleaded guilty to only one of the six charges against him, claiming he had helped Hammond to escape only to protect his clients, who weren't then charged, from possible blackmail. The Attorney General accepted Newton's pleas and didn't present any evidence on the other five charges.

However, on 20 May, the presiding judge sentenced Newton to six weeks in prison, then widely thought by the legal profession to be rather harsh. A petition which had been signed by 250 London law firms was then sent to the Home Secretary, Henry Matthews, protesting at Newton's treatment.

All those subsequent leads which were investigated by police failed to produce much more evidence against the suspects and the aristocratic gentlemen, like Somerset and his companions, had by then disappeared, as it were, into thin air. So also unresolved was the mystery of the Prince of Wales son's presence there, Albert Victor Eddie. He had been seen by some of the suspects as present in the brothel but had apparently escaped before the police began their interviews and were able to complete their investigation.

As a result, and partly because of the furore which arose in the newspapers of the time, the Cleveland St Scandal ended as thoroughly confused as it began, with no real proof or hope by detectives that the Prince Albert Eddy could ever be prosecuted, even if they had the evidence to do so, which is unlikely, since most of the evidence against him was simply circumstantial. And circumstantial evidence, as Sherlock Holmes would have known, is highly unsatisfactory, without some empirical evidence also being produced with which to back it up.

Somerset himself escaped to France and thence travelled to Europe and America, and he was never brought to the courts in person to account for his offences, apart from the inconvenience of paying high legal fees to his solicitor. The fact that the two leading boys involved in the conspiracy also were given short prison sentences was yet another unsatisfactory component of the issue. The whole affair of the Cleveland Street Scandal certainly does demonstrate how very vulnerable and open to corruption young boys were, particularly on the street, even when pursuing an apparently legitimate lifestyle or occupation.

There is, to my mind, not a shadow of a doubt that the Duke of Clarence was embroiled in this affair and that others, principally Lord Somerset, were prepared to suffer the punishment meted out to them for their exploitation of young boys.

But could it also have been the case that the man seen leaving the male brothel in Cleveland Street with Lord Somerset was not the Duke of Clarence, after all, but was in fact, Montague Druitt?

To extend the conspiracy theory even further, is it possible that since Montague and the Duke of Clarence bore what I can only describe as an uncanny resemblance to each other, the royal family then used him as a doppelgänger; then, either incarcerating or killing the Duke in order to protect the reputation and integrity of Victoria. Thus, by this nefarious plot, they would be able to keep the reputation of the royal family intact. It seems a rather wild conspiracy theory and yet I find myself attracted to it.

Printed in Great Britain
by Amazon